THE REVIEW *of* CONTEMPORARY FICTION

THE FUTURE OF BRITISH FICTION

FALL 2012 / VOL. XXXII, NO.3

EDITOR

JOHN O'BRIEN

ASSOCIATE EDITOR

IRVING MALIN

GUEST EDITORS

PATRICIA WAUGH

JENNIFER HODGSON

MANAGING EDITOR

JEREMY M. DAVIES

PRODUCTION

LAURA COLGAN

PROOFREADER

NATALIE HAMILTON

INTERN

KATHERINE NEWPORT

REVIEW OF CONTEMPORARY FICTION
Fall 2012
Vol. XXXII, No. 3

The *Review of Contemporary Fiction* is published three times each year
(March, August, November). Subscription prices are as follows:

Single volume (three issues):
Individuals: $17.00 U.S.; $22.60 Canada; $32.60 all other countries
Institutions: $26.00 U.S.; $31.60 Canada; $41.60 all other countries

ISSN: 0276-0045
ISBN: 978-1-56478-892-4

Partially funded by a grant from the Illinois Arts Council, a state agency, and by
the University of Illinois at Urbana-Champaign

Indexed in *Humanities International Complete, International Bibliography of Periodical Literature, International Bibliography of Book Reviews, MLA Bibliography*, and *Book Review Index.*
Abstracted in *Abstracts of English Studies.*

The *Review of Contemporary Fiction* is also available on 16mm microfilm, 35mm microfilm, and
105mm microfiche from University Microfilms International, 300 North Zeeb Road, Ann Arbor,
MI 48106-1346.

Address all correspondence to:
Review of Contemporary Fiction
University of Illinois
1805 S. Wright Street, MC-011
Champaign, IL 61820

Cover photo: Jamie George

www.dalkeyarchive.com

THE REVIEW OF CONTEMPORARY FICTION

BACK ISSUES AVAILABLE

Back issues are still available for the following numbers of the *Review of Contemporary Fiction* ($8 each unless otherwise noted):

Individuals receive a 10% discount on orders of one issue and a 20% discount on orders of two or more issues. To place an order, use the form on the last page of this issue.

CONTENTS

THE REVIEW *of* CONTEMPORARY FICTION

PATRICIA WAUGH AND JENNIFER HODGSON

Introduction

This issue of the *Review of Contemporary Fiction* is, for the first time, devoted to—but not devotional towards—British contemporary fiction. Over its thirty-year history, the *Review* has already done a fine job of airing out the back bedroom of book culture in the UK. Literary outliers, otherwise viewed as a kind of Shandyean digression from the master-plot of British literary history, have found some sanctuary within its pages: 'minor' novelists of the sixties such as B.S. Johnson, Alan Burns, Ann Quin, Nicholas Mosley, or the category-defying writers of the forties such as Henry Green and Elizabeth Bowen. But look in the pages of the *Review* and from around the early seventies you might infer the arrival of a new dark age, a strange blight on the literary-fictional landscape: British writing seems to drop off the page. With the exception of a few bright interludes, the writing of Kazuo Ishiguro and Alasdair Gray, for example, that forty year old cloud still hangs. Committed to bringing innovative writing to wider attention, the *Review* has its work cut out locating any on this side of the Atlantic. Listen also to the response of one British writer, currently feted in academic Europhile circles, to our invitation to write about the new fiction in Britain; on declining, he confessed: 'I'm not sure I have anything to say. I didn't know there was any'. Disingenuous hauteur or self-possessed national self-dispossession? Is this now ritualised disavowal of the new merely an empty but unexamined myth ripe for explosion, or are there real but more intractable problems in nurturing innovative fictional writing in Britain? If so, do the problems lie with the writing, the perception of the writing, or with the national culture that frames production and reception of the writing? Or do the problems begin somewhere else altogether? Our refusenik jabbed his index finger at the problem and then shrugged his shoulders and walked away. Did he wish to deny his own status as an innovator, or his identity as British, or is he the self-styled exception that proves the rule?

In a culture where all too often literary 'innovation' is read as 'degeneration', where the experimental novelist is viewed as a case of narcissistic personality disorder, and where the new is identified with a 'creeping' cosmopolitanism that dilutes the local produce, the very idea of British innovative fiction comes to sound like an *oxymoronic* supplement—a kind of pharmakon—to the idea of the *moronic* inferno. Though postmodernism only ever reared its head disguised as a kind of indigenous contested empiricism—like arguments for the existence of the Loch Ness monster or Tony Blair's sincerity—its spectral afterlife is now a source for lingering embarrassment within literary academia: pomo sold out, went commercial, went moronic, got down with the dodgier intimates of the inferno. Academic literary critics attempting to push the case for a rejuvenated new British novel tend to side-step the problem of the oxy and are anxious to avoid being tarred by the moronic. So they reframe the new in the terms of someplace or sometime or something else, most often the 'neo-modern' or the 'late modern' or the 'anxiously modern'. Or they have a field day with riffs on the 'new realism': hysterical, hyper-, contested, problematised, paranoid and dirty—but hardly ever *contemporary*. Peter Ackroyd wrote in 2001 about the way in which British novelists were now beginning to present reality as 'uncomfortable, as being demanding . . . less open to conventional habits of narration and description' and about how we are 'continually being made aware of the oddness of the ordinary, the menace and brutality which is behind the conventional political and social worlds'. Groping for a suitable nomenclature to append to the new writing, however, he ends lamely, albeit with characteristic disavowal of ownership: 'You might, I suppose, call it the new realism—paranoid realism'. Soft-centred liberals all, we British seem shackled either to the safety of the ready-made category, or the already canonised, or to the comfortably quotidian. Our peculiar creed is mortally suspicious of untrammelled aestheticism, endlessly asserting the primacy of content over form. In accounts of British writing, even now—long after such a thing could be anything other than a rather quaint anachronism of an old culture war—the avant-garde features as a kind of bogeyman. One whose dandified aestheticism belies a questionable politics, a moral compass gone awry; who must be beaten back by decency and common sense. Literary experiment still tends to be perceived as a pernicious form of French 'flu: of course we should still be *bloody grateful* for the English Channel, separating, as it does, steady, dependable old Blighty from *that kind of thing*.

At the very moment of writing this introduction, the British government is huddled behind closed doors, debating a new immigration bill that will require those seeking permanent residency in Britain to pass an examination in Shakespeare, Dickens and Hardy. Without intending to revive the old chestnut of British cultural studies of the eighties—all those arguments about the national culture and the avowed 'greatness' of Shakespeare, Dickens and Hardy as Arnoldian touchstones of value—we still feel a weary kind of bafflement that official sanction should once again be given to the idea that learning a soundbite Shakespearean chakra might offer a quick route to cultural assimilation, or to what is considered most vigorous and valuable about living in a new as well as an old country. Is that really the best they can do? A mercantilist visionary, a nineteenth-century Christian humanist, an agrarian fin-de-siecle melancholic? But we no longer live even in an age of mechanical reproduction. We live in a post-industrial, neo-corporate, trans-national world of globalised forces where locating yourself in the particularities of a specific time and place requires more than rote learning the decontextualised soundbites of the English literary tradition. Contemporary Britain, like the United States and the nations of Europe and Asia is now a country with complex interconnections across the globe, through the circuits of international finance, the networks of the new corporate governance and management, and the social networks of the new media. Some of our newest fiction negotiates a path through this entanglement of the local and the global with exuberant style, phenomenological sensitivity, and an almost forensic eye for the way in which experiential nuances of imagination, perception, memory and dream are all also shaped by a culture, a place and a moment and memory. Shakespeare is not the only British inventor of New Worlds. As Hilary Mantel insists: 'If you want to write about the "state of the nation", you have to study dreams and nightmares, as well as returns from opinion polls. You can't omit the emotional and the irrational'. If you are looking to understand Britain now, you might put down *Henry V* and set aside for a moment *Tess of the D'Urbervilles*. You might perhaps linger over *Hard Times*, but we recommend that you move on and read Nicola Barker's *Darkmans*, or Hilary Mantel's *Beyond Black* or Jonathan Coe's *The Terrible Privacy of Maxwell Sim* or J.G. Ballard's *Super-Cannes* or Tom McCarthy's *Remainder* or John McGregor's *If Nobody Speaks of Remarkable Things* or Jim Crace's *The Pesthouse*. This special issue is dedicated to examining some of these writers and assumptions.

The British writer-critic James Wood, now distinguished Harvard professor and unacknowledged legislator of the fiefdom of contemporary fiction, has done much to consolidate the history of British literary fictional decline. Initially drawing useful ballast from Hugh Kenner's lament for a 'sinking island' after the demise of literary Modernism, his trans-Atlantic prognostications drew further scaffolding from post-colonial critics' version of the Great Aetiolation. Jed Esty has written the best known account, but in framing it as yet another Empire Writes Back story, he places any reader in the inevitably compromised position of seeming, churlishly, to Write Back to an Empire That is Writing Back, and seeming, therefore, to collude with Empire. One of the official histories of the retreat from heroic, *British* ocean-going ambition, the Imperialist triumphalism anatomised in Conrad's *Heart of Darkness*, Esty's account sees Imperial greatness now stranded in a stagnant backwater, a kind of Kenneth Grahame messing about on the river, with Ratty, Badger and Mole, dabbling with the ducks in the safe rivulets of *English* pastoral. In this account, Forsterian lyrical realism established itself as *the* British Way of Fiction by turning British into English. Though Forster may have barely registered the sinking and the shrinkage of the nation in 1910, he noted all too well that its hub, its capital, floated vertiginously on a 'sea of porridge' thickened with foreign capital. Forster's answer was to exchange the hub for the heart and to recommend a quiet nativist retreat to the English Country House, the village pageant, with a dash of Pagan or Gothic mystery, and the occasional hint of German Romanticism. Zadie Smith, kicking her heels on the way to the Atlantic, recently paid homage to the vision in her transatlantic novel, *On Beauty*. A caricature, of course. Yet the Kenner-Wood-Esty case is curiously borne out in unlikely places. There is abundant evidence that our innovative writers—in a softer version of Eliotic European-Christian-Greco-Buddhist re-fashioning—have collaborated with it, seeming to need psychologically to eschew the allegiances and associations of 'Britishness' or 'Englishness' and to assert the innovator aspect of their identities through self-conscious association with the Continental or the Transatlantic: one thinks here not only of Eliot's editorship of *The Criterion*, but of Murdoch's homage to Queneau and Beckett in her first novel; Trocchi and Brooke-Rose's love affair with French intellectual culture; Spark's with the Catholicism of Maritain rather than Newman; A.S. Byatt's avowal of herself as a European; Martin Amis's love-hate relationship with America and American writers such as Bellow and Roth; Zadie Smith's aforementioned looking back through the lens of all things cross-Atlantic (hip-hop, rap and David Foster Wallace). Similar tendencies are evident in some of the most interesting and vigorous new writers such as Tom McCarthy whose novels resonate with the Beckettian, the phenomenological and the existential, or in Alan Hollinghurst and Adam Thirlwell, who embrace an aristocratic, Euro-transatlantic lineage of James and Nabokov, Edmund White and Milan Kundera. Without exception, of course, all these self-avowedly 'cosmopolitan' writers marry with and promiscuously blend the foreign with the indigenous, the international with the demotic—but what seems to fix their identity in their own eyes and ours is their avowed association with cultures and traditions that are not British.

Interestingly, many of the writers discussed or appearing in this edition seem to be in recovery or to be getting over the hang-up: they borrow and read and allude with ease to what Rushdie refers to as the 'sea of stories' and they write happily of the Isle of Dogs, of Shepperton, of Luton, the London Orbital, the East End, the lowlands and blackened wastelands of the industrialised Midlands, lives lived in back to back streets, on New Build Infotechland estates, remote Scottish islands, and the endless out-of-town shopping malls of the New Britain. This *is* a marked change to the seventies. Take for example Kazuo Ishiguro's oft-pronounced sense of the difficulties of escaping the provincialism of British fiction in that decade, the feeling of Britain's increasing marginalisation in world-politics, a geographic isolationism so evident that it seemed impossible to imagine that literary value could not be part of the general 'shrinkage'. British writers felt that the Big Events were happening elsewhere; interesting fiction was bound to follow; the balance of powers was shifting. His own novel *The Unconsoled* of 1996 was a brilliant rendition of the dangers and seductions of 'going International' as a way of escaping this threat of parochialism (interestingly also the theme too of Adam Thirlwell's more recent novel of that name). *The Unconsoled* is a psychomachia of the newly professionalised cosmopolitan artist struggling to maintain a fierce public relations 'schedule' with pressures on him to perform his art and exercise a telescopic ambassadorial philanthropy. On yet another tour, he finds himself in a strange space of nowhere, an international hotel, in an unnamed place, at an unnamed time, somewhere in the middle of Europe. He wrestles too with a landscape awash with material projections of his own autobiographical memories, fantasies, dreams and fears. Surely a figure for the new professionalised and internationalised writer, Ryder bumps up against the ghosts of his past and the buried and split-off alters of himself, in a landscape built out of hints and glimpses of *The Waste Land*, *Ariadne on Naxos*, Escher's drawings, the films of Bergman and the Coen brothers, German Romanticism, Nietzsche and Freud, the traditions of the *Mittel-European Volk*.

Modernism has frequently been invoked as the straw man of a wider British distrust of intellectualism. See, for instance, John Carey's conspiracy theorising about the Moderns' snobbery and their intellectual pretensions in his *The Intellectuals and the Masses* (1992). Gabriel Josipovici's recent *kulturpessimismus* polemic, *What Ever Happened to Modernism?*, condemns a buttoned-up Englishry that he sees as dreary and anecdotal, unable to distinguish between reality and *l'effet de reel*; one that has consistently misunderstood the modernist project. But part of the problem for the serious literary novelist in Britain has actually often been the difficulty of getting over Modernism. Not just as a problem of production, but one of reception too. The new experimental writer was once almost inevitably going to be dubbed the new Beckett or Kafka or Joyce. Once modernism was set up as introspective and concerned with the 'dark places of psychology', to use Woolf's description, writers of the forties like Green, Bowen and Compton-Burnett saw the challenge as finding a way to eschew the assumed 'inward turn' in order to create worlds through dialogue, expressionist rendition, behaviourist technique and phenomenologies of perception that blurred memory and perception, inner and outer voices, hierarchies of narration.

Crucial to this was the intuitive novelistic recognition (spelt out later, philosophically, by both Sartre and Merleau-Ponty) already powerful in Bowen and Green, that feeling is not always, most often not in fact, felt; feeling is most often experienced as the feeling-tone or mood that seems more the attribute of a world or a scene: the vibrancy of backlighting, shadows, edges, colours, the rhythm and pace of a world made in words. Perception is style, as Martin Amis has insisted, but perception is also style that unconceals, tacitly and obliquely, a world and, through a process of reverse introjection, a self. That the world exists for me as my world and that I exist for myself, is what Sartre refers to as *ipseity*. The feeling that I don't exist, the loss of a tacit sense of self-presence, that I don't inhabit my body or the world, is the feeling-tone pervasive in fiction since the seventies but first captured as part of a new inhospitable and corporate world in Camus' *The Stranger*. Meursault cannot feel at all, but his world is conveyed through one of the most powerful and distinctive 'feeling-tones' in modern fiction (Amis, incidentally, uses the word in *Time's Arrow* in a similar attempt to write the Nazi soul). This mode of disconnection in its blank, or hyper-reflexive, or comically disjunctive form—that begins with Dostoevsky, Kafka, Musil and Beckett—has been a major orientation of twentieth-century literary fiction in Britain, but barely remarked in the general preoccupation with making fine discriminations between realism, and modernism and late modernism and postmodernism.

It is the very self-consciously executed *modus vivendi* of McCarthy's *Remainder*. Take the *Watt*-like scene with the carrot in the physiotherapy clinic: 'I closed my fingers round the carrot. It felt—well, it *felt*; that was enough to start short-circuiting the operation. It had texture; it had mass. The whole week I'd been gearing up to lift it, I'd thought of my hands, my fingers, my rerouted brain as active agents, and the carrot as a nothing—a hollow, a carved space for me to grasp and move. This carrot though, was more active than me: the way it bumped and wrinkled; how it crawled with grit'. Like Ryder, this protagonist is another who conceives of himself as an artist; this novel too—like Ishiguro's *Never Let Me Go* or Mantel's *Beyond Black* or Hollinghurst's less overtly experimental *The Line of Beauty* or Smith's *On Beauty*—is a disquisition on the place of art in a commodified world. Here a Platonic intentionality—but it could as well be Romantic—attempts to materialise its vision through various corporate networks of facilitation and, in the process, exposes the dangerous and mechanistic splitting of mind, body, and world that lurks in the Platonic and the Cartesian and is now generalised over Britain in the corporate world of reality management. McCarthy's twenty-first-century Frankenstein inhabits and acts out a hyper-reflexive world of 'cool' where money is able to hire an army of networked agents, project managers and special-effects workers specialised in the materialisation of corporate 'vision' as the already confabulated memories viewed as the remaining source of the idea of a soul. Like Ishiguro's, McCarthy's novel too is also about fiction as compensation—a settlement—that undoes itself as it points up all those losses and holes in the real. It is a world where performance is all, and weariness, the weariness of the self, has long set in; where a Beckettian akrasia is now a circuit-disconnect between wiring and neurotransmission in the brain and wiring and neurotransmission to the muscles of the body. It is a world where the pre-reflexive has been almost entirely replaced by the management of the event and the orchestrated confabulation of the 'real' as memory, dream and perception. *Remainder* has made its mark, perhaps, because it so exquisitely connects the metafictional with the neo-corporate with our revived interest in the phenomenology of perception and imagination and feeling. How does a novelist preserve the anagnosia that is at the heart of practical daily living, the tacit knowing that eludes language? How do you do it in words? And how do you use those words to expose a world where words have been betrayed into the service of a coercive management and production of a kind of emptied out real: the new management protocols of event production, performance monitoring and the corporate scripting of the real as 'cool'? Perhaps the really new realism is that we turn to fiction to experience the feeling of the real. And that takes us somehow beyond the postmodern.

In our obsessions with modernism, postmodernism, realism, neomodernism, late modernism, the hysterical, the paranoid, the hyper- and the ever 'new' realism, perhaps we have forgotten that a major strength of the British novel has always lain in this kind of phenomenological, often semi-expressionist rendition and self-conscious rehearsal of the building and dismantling of imaginary worlds and the fabulation of a sense of the real. It is there in Sterne's ironic laying bare of the sentimentalist claims for the novel at the beginning of the era of political economy, or in Woolf's dissemination of mind through the complex representation of phenomenologies of perception, memory and imagination, or in Muriel Spark's wicked way of estranging us from our lived and assumed modes of estrangement as she takes a willed detour round the sentimental to restore us to a proper empathy with the poor, the marginalised and excluded. Without this altered perception of literary history, the fifties will continue to be written up as a disappointing and unambitious return to or collapse back into middle of the road social realism: ignoring the surrealism of A.L. Barker, the comic and haunting expressionism of late Green, the hyper-reflexive strangeness of *The Aerodrome*, the Tourettish and grotesque mimicry that makes up much of *Lucky Jim*, the Wittgensteinian reflection on and enaction of solipsism that is *Pincher Martin*, the dispersed, disconnected consciousness that engages the experience of factory life in Sillitoe's *Saturday Night and Sunday Morning*, or the comic suburban grotesque of William Sansom's brilliant novel, *The Body*. Writers such as Beryl Bainbridge, Doris Lessing, early McEwan, Murdoch, Spark, Ballard, Kelman, Burgess, all cut their teeth as part of this trajectory; the legacy extends to McCarthy, Mantel, Barker and many of the writers featured in these pages.

To accept this alternative picture is surely to take on board the possibility that there are outward-looking but native traditions of experiment that exceed the usual accounts of the so-called inward turn of modernism, or the turning inside out of fictional convention in the postmodern, or the insider-outsider, Empire Writes Back, double perspectivism of the post-colonial. There is a native version of phenomenology and it flourishes in our fiction; surrealism, expressionism and blankness rub along with comic extravagance, linguistic exuberance and a Todorovian kind of fantastic happily mingling natural with supernatural and the spiritual and transcendental with the weird and wacky. And yet, the story of the decline of the nation tacked onto the fortunes of the novel, the academic obsession with historical and stylistic placing and cate-gorisation, even a kind of lingering Leavisism that sees art primarily as a guide to the moral or the good life, all create problems for the perception, reception and encouragement of aesthetic newness in Britain. The self-induced dispos-session of national identity so marked in our literary culture seems, well, *Brit-ish*. And it often feels remarkably difficult to avoid the self-fulfilling pressure of the stereotype. Turn to the American writer, Jonathan Franzen's recent apo-logia for his own style of autobiographical fiction, for example, and there's no hint of such identity problems: 'When I write', he says, I don't feel like a craftsman influenced by earlier craftsmen who were themselves influenced by earlier craftsmen. I feel like a member of a single, large virtual community in which I have dynamic relationships with other members of the community, most of whom are no longer living. As in any other community, I have my friends and I have my enemies. I find my way to the corners of the world of fiction where I feel most at home, most securely but also provocatively among my friends'. Franzen's place is comfortably globe-trotting round the worlds of fiction in his head: the world of fiction as a world of story-worlds and not promotional tours, publicity launches and national book culture.

But a question remains, perhaps, whether there was actually a falling off in the seventies from which things never recovered. Did interesting and inno-vative British fiction really succumb entirely—as the various accounts would have it—to the inclement climate of British late consumer culture, the New Philistinism, the dumbing down of a compromised welfare consensus, the paralysing legacy of modernist brilliance or the loss of Empire and national pride? In a now infamous editorial (of 1993) to the literary magazine, *Granta*, Bill Buford blamed the word 'British' itself for poisoning the wells of talent: 'a grey, unsatisfactory, bad-weather kind of word, a piece of linguistic compromise'. In a landscape (then) beginning to seem more refreshed by the voices of the trans-national, the migrant and the diasporic, the idea of 'British', however, for Buford, seemed to hang in the air like a toxic miasma, stymieing progress and the cultivation of the new. 'British' was a bad spell; no longer a description of the real. 'I still don't know anyone who is British. I know people who are English or Scottish or Northern Irish (not to mention born in Nigeria but living here or born-in-London of Pakistani parents and living here . . . or born-in-Nigeria- but-living here-Nigerian-English) '. But Buford too (also an American) now seems strangely hung up on the Kenner account, convinced that the only means of renewal still depended on Imperial powers, now in reverse as the Empire Wrote Back.

Though there is no necessary connection between the luminosity of events in history and the significance and value of artistic representation, literary critics seem curiously attached to this view of things. They are driven perhaps by different concerns than writers themselves, concerns to do with historical placing, cultural trajectories, political interventions, real or imagined, and less so with the nitty-gritty of that incredibly difficult task of imagining and making a world. If we literary critics thought more like novelists and less like historians or sociologists, perhaps we might begin to see that the fifties consisted of more than Angry Young Men or deferential genuflections in bicycle clips. Perhaps we might begin to do justice to the immensely variegated and innovatory work of that decade and perhaps we might see the fifties is a good place to begin to explode the Kenner and Co. myth of inevitable decline? Similarly, perhaps, the 1980s had more on offer than a political imagination fired up by Margaret Thatcher or the Empire Writing Back or Lyotard's critique of metanarratives. Perhaps even the 1970s, as the Age of No Style, had styles that awaited a hermeneutic imagination more attuned to factories than flares, ghosts than governments, Granny rock than Glam rock (Beryl Bainbridge's *The Bottle Factory Outing* perhaps as against Martin Amis's *The Pregnant Widow*). Writers are freer than critics to ignore the strictures of periodisation, the interminable debates about location and positioning. They can stick their necks out more freely—aren't they meant to?—without alienating an 'interpretive community' or being excluded from the academic Research Exercise—the six yearly cull of academic 'research' imposed by a national government stingy on higher ed. funding but generous to the point of silliness with the provision of League Tables: 'I've never understood the categorisation of postcolonial writing. I've been sent papers where I'm talked about as a postcolonial novelist, but I'm never sure about the definition. Does 'postcolonial' mean writing that came out in the postcolonial era? Or does it have to come from a country that used to be part of an empire, and which, after the colonies started to devolve, changed into an independent state? Or does it mean writing by people who don't have white skins . . . Whether somebody is postcolonial seems to be defined by the writer's biography rather than by their writing, and that's what makes me very suspicious of postcolonial writing as a category'. Ishiguro voices something often obscurely felt but ne'er so well expressed—or, more likely, ne'er dared to be expressed, at least by academic critics forced to keep one eye on political and the other on professional correctness. What if novels *are* primarily now read as ways out of loneliness as Jonathan Franzen has recently averred? Does that make them less difficult to write? Or less political? Doesn't that entail trying to understand and find ways to represent, analyse and imaginatively transform the sources of our sense of contemporary disaffection or lack of or skewed affect? Historicisation in fiction is rooted in the singularity of a storyworld, created through a process of formal imagination and craft. If we make fiction 'piggyback' too much on history, as Ishiguro suggests later in the same interview (2012), 'it leads to the preservation of mediocre books whilst some brilliant books are forgotten because they don't fit the clear historical model'. Sometimes new mutations, hopeful monsters, struggling to push their way out of blighted soil are trodden over by the love affair with historical frames or correctness. There is a brilliant image of this kind of erasure in Hilary Mantel's weirdly evocative *Beyond Black*. Alison, the protagonist, is a 'sensitive', an artiste soothsayer in the lucrative futures market of housewifely depression that is spawning across the info-tech, city commuter, suburban hinterlands of the 'redeveloped' London orbital. Conurbative sprawl unfurls the distressed Georgian facades and the bright nursery acrylics that serve as camouflage for the loss of history and the loss of hope. The new breed of professionalised mediums and New Age therapists, with their business cards and aftercare customer services plans, swoop like vultures, plying their wares and simples for the sick modern soul, making over, going over, passing over. Alison endlessly communes with the dead of her own past, listening to the voices of a traumatic childhood, pushed, pummelled and poked by familiar ghosts, somatic pains and tortures. She needs her trade, her 'profession' of medium (another figure for the contemporary artist) as the means of self-therapy. But egged on by her 'business' partner, Colette, trained up as an Events Manager, she is encouraged to Aim Higher and Think Big. She buys a New Build on an infotech and city commuter estate that Colette sees as 'investment' more than home, a pension pot in a world that is unremittingly future. But staring into the foundations of the as yet unbuilt house, gifted with what she refers to as 'hearsight', Alison hear-sees much more: that 'roar' of silence from the other side of this middle distance and middle England real, that haunted George Eliot in her own nineteenth century tale of middle England but from which she shudderingly drew back. Not so Mantel: 'Now she stood looking about her. She sensed the underscape, shuddering as it waited to be ripped. Builders machines stood ready, their maws crusted with soil, waiting for Monday morning. Violence hung in the air, like the smell of explosive. Birds had flown. Foxes had abandoned their lairs. The bones of mice and voles were mulched into mud, and she sensed the minute snapping of frail necks and the grinding into paste of muscle and fur. Through the soles of her shoes she felt gashed worms turning, twisting and repairing themselves . . . She could see ghost horses, huddled in the shadow of a wall. It was an indifferent place; no better nor worse than most others.'

Yet, despite the successive incursions of threads, pockets and outcroppings of the experimental and the reality of a more variegated literary history than 'official' accounts almost always offer, the mainstream picture of the British novel is still dominated by the idea of a time-worn 'English style'. Colm Tóibín recently characterised the 'quintessential English novel of our age' as 'well made, low on ambition and filled with restraint, taking its bearings from a world that Philip Larkin made in his own image.' Zadie Smith, in 'Two Paths for the Novel' speculates on the future of fiction in English by way of reviews of novels by latter-day realist, Joseph O'Neill, and of Tom McCarthy as the great white hope for British avant-garde writing. She finds O'Neill's is the road most travelled. His 'breed of lyrical Realism' (there we go again) has 'had the freedom of the highway for some time now, with most other exits blocked'. Although Smith specifies the Anglophone novel, her view seems more narrowly applicable to fiction in Britain. And we've had the good grace to export this ethic in the views of James Wood, 'the finest literary critic writing in English today,' (as is customary to append). Wood is deeply mistrustful even of the company kept by Smith herself, those hip young gunslingers that congregate around McSweeney's and *The Believer*. His pleas for reason and decency against a pervasive American fetish for vulgar stylistics, for those 'very 'brilliant' books which know a thousand things but do not know a single human being', issue weekly from the pages of *The New Yorker*. For in Britain, where, as we've seen, the state of the novel is more likely to be closely pegged to the state of the nation, fiction has been obliged to provide a repository for stable truths and social order. 'Englishness' (very rarely 'Britishness') has remained a major preoccupation in our fictions. Novels have long been burdened with providing the sense of spiritual coherence that social commentators insist we so sorely lack despite, or, in fact, because of, an increasingly dispersed and devolved national culture. This, the summer of the British monarch's Diamond Jubilee and the London Olympics has tested an uneasy, class conscious, and ambivalent relationship with a nationalism reinterpreted as national pride and belonging that many British people are still loathe to admit. This year's celebrations follow on from the previous summer's outbreak of violence, raids, looting and riots that saw major areas of the city of London in flames. Interspersed with BBC coverage of Wimbledon, a new Shakespeare season and pictures of the Olympic torch on its progress round the towns of Britain are documentaries and narratives of the mostly 16-24 year-old rioters now released from prison and facing life with disabling criminal convictions. As for nationalism, as Stefan Collini writes, we seem always to have insisted that such a primitive—and historically troublesome—impulse is something that happens elsewhere. Nationalism has long been a vexed issue here. The World War II-era injunction to 'Keep Calm and Carry On' has become the atavistic mantra of Recession Britain visible everywhere from towels to teacups. It appeals to our mythic image of ourselves; the 'blitz spirit' with which we might weather this new Age of Austerity. But as our 'collective symbol' the Union Jack has an uncomfortable double existence. It is similarly, 'harmless' pageantry, a Little England party favour, but it is also historically loaded and queasily evocative, making us instinctively—and often unquestioningly—uneasy.

We have not lost our mania for manifesting the particularity (and the peculiarity) of being English. The metaphysics of Eliot and Leavis might have gone lukewarm for many and stone cold for most, but we still continue to attempt to conjure a coherent whole from less than the sum of its parts. But smoggy mill towns, red pillar boxes and fried breakfasts of an English particularist like Orwell have, however, given way to rather more ersatz assemblages. The cover of the recent Britain-themed issue of *Granta* depicts a chipped bone china teacup with its handle wrenched off. This, neatly, is the 'Broken Britain' of tabloid and Tory parlance. The nation recorded within is peopled with desperate pen-pushers, small-time dealers of recreational pharmaceuticals, missing children, Eastern European lap dancers and timorous lower-league footballers with Lady Chatterley-esque designs upon the groundsman. It's an urban-pastoral hinterland, hung with a murder-scene gloaming of incipient menace. Abandoned old-New Towns and sink estates, the condemned edifices of post-war utopian dreaming—and of local government corruption—feature heavily. So, too, does a British state of mind governed by shame, repression and lassitude and given to random and not-so-random acts of violence.

Yet it with these ingredients, the poet and novelist John Burnside argues, that we might put Britain, like Humpty Dumpty, back together again. '[H]ome, or identity', he suggests, 'can be found in cultural ruins.' Britain might be, as self-styled alternative poet laureate Simon Armitage has it, reduced to a 'shipwreck's carcass' and 'down to its bare bones', but with the loss of 'old certainties' comes the loosening of the old hierarchies too, and with it the possibility for remodelling Britain along more democratic, more egalitarian lines. This, for Burnside, is cause for a 'tender, if guarded, celebration':

> To recognise the new values that emerge from the makeshift is to discover the earliest traces of a new direction, the first tentative steps in a spontaneous remaking of ourselves, the hazy outline of a democratising order that imagination finds in the unlikeliest of places.

But is this really the cause for (albeit cautious) jubilation? Should a 'sense of identity' really come at such a cost? And is celebration really the most appropriate response? *Granta*'s picture of Britain is not, as it purports to be, an unflinchingly democratic picture of a diverse society, but the finessing of a poverty of many kinds into the picturesque; the requisite local colour now provided by all those on-the-bones-of-their-arse Britons.

Burnside seems at once to under- and over-estimate what art can do. We might now be rather more sceptical about the real-world capabilities of the artistic imagination to ameliorate social injustice. And we might question how effective a model of egalitarianism narrative fiction can be. The iconography of this 'Broken Britain' is well on its way to becoming a collection of clichés of 'Englishness' that is just as politically malign, cosy and self-satisfied than the old one. Burnside's is, at least, a very British sentiment: It might be *crap* but at least it's *ours*. For Martin Amis, on the other hand, the appropriate response to a country he recently declaimed for its 'moral decrepitude' is satire. His new 'State of England' novel, *Lionel Asbo,* is a parting shot as Amis absconds for America. 'Who let the dogs in?' the epigraph asks, in the first of many woefully misjudged (and woefully out-of-date) pop culture references. In the novel, Amis romances Britain's underclass into a coterie of grotesques that are at once Jerry Springer-generic and farcically bizarre: the single mothers, illiterate bruisers and petty criminals are joined by a glamour model-slash-aspiring poetess, pitbulls raised on Tabasco. The response has been almost unanimously negative; unsurprising since, as once reviewer commented, Amis' novel amounts to little more than narrative-as-trolling.

Fellow novelist Nicola Barker has been a rare voice in defence of *Lionel Asbo*, arguing, in her review, that 'maybe modern England needs offending'. She maintains that thin-skinned Britons might well need this kind of baiting to shake them from their cosy, tea-and-biscuits slumber. Surprising, this, from Barker, since although she was recently puffed as the 'female Martin Amis', her own novels engage with the 'reality' of living in Britain (*whatever that might mean*, her fictions always insist on appending) with an authenticity and a sensitivity rarely seen in Amis'. Far from proffering a searing critique of the state of the nation, Barker's so-called progenitor appears to be in cahoots with a culture that is, in terms of its cruelty and vacuity, already way beyond the poison of his pen. See for example, the ritualised humiliations of über-franchised reality television or even more so our government, whose economic policymaking in the face of the global economic recession evinces a level of care and sympathy more often seen in the S&M parlour, or indeed, in the public school fagging system with which PM David Cameron is so familiar. 'We' (who, *us*?) have been decadent, chastise the swingeing cuts initiated by the coalition government, and now, inevitably, *we must be punished*.

It is customary, at this juncture, to segue effortlessly into tentative optimism. To defer to the 'complexity' of the situation. To issue disclaimers about the partial view of our presentism. To talk of 'green shoots' and 'possibilities'. And this issue is, in a sense, no exception. Innovative and ambitious novels continue to be written in Britain; there might be more of them, and those that there are might be better known, if only there was someone to vouch for them. Literary criticism, once envisioned by F. R. Leavis as the 'humane centre' of British culture, long since split into the factions of Grub Street and Ivory Tower, and there has been little love lost between the two since Leavis's heyday. Reacting against this ethical burden, the British literary academy was a keen late adapter to continental theory. Over-eager, in fact; for it was soon accused by novelists of having all but abandoned the novel, having thrown the baby out with the bath water of Leavis and the New Criticism. This caricature of academe is, at least in part, the product of a long-standing British mistrust of 'Theory'. Yet who could blame literary academics for sexing up the British novel with liberal applications of cool, continental philosophy on hot topics like death and desire; or those who manage to divine an encounter with the Lacanian Real in the po-faced sex-farce (sometimes labelled 'neo-Victorian') of Ian McEwan's *On Chesil Beach*? But in this era of impact-assessment and quota-fulfilment, the academy's attempts to grapple with the British contemporary novel have often felt like a will-this-do concession to relevance. Perhaps it would be better advised to modify its attempts to validate its objects of study by overburdening them with demands for relevance to political or government correctness and simply try to lift the longstanding taboo on aesthetic evaluation that might lend its weight to, well, better novels.

The literary press in Britain has eagerly taken up the Leavisite slack, moonlighting as the moral advocate of the self-consciously middlebrow. It exists as the heavily-subsidised, loss-making adjuncts and supplements to newspapers, with the exception of the *London Review of Books*, funded by its editor's family trust. The little magazines and periodicals of other book cultures (and of poetry) do not exist in any significant number here, surprising given the boon of the internet to such an enterprise. Perhaps because of this, as with so much cultural life in Britain, our literary press is all too aware of a public service remit, but is by no means sure of whom its audience might comprise. It addresses an Ideal Reader that is both unapologetically philistine and impossibly highfalutin'. That likes its books 'serious' and 'weighty', but not 'dry' or 'obscure' and certainly never to 'lack heart'. That wants its ethical heuristics trussed up in majestically lyrical prose. Here—where novels are breathlessly praised for their skilful navigation of our twenty-first-century dilemmas and for the delicate craft of their storytelling—lies what used to be called literary fiction in Britain. E.M. Forster need not have worried about the fate of his 'little society'—it is alive and well, at least in the pages of the literary press.

Whilst British literary critics are reverential about the innate value of the (definite article, capital letter) Novel, they remain wholly unconvinced about the broader possibilities of fictional narrative. See, for example, Liam McIlva-nney and Ray Ryan's take on the 'novelness' of novels in *The Good of the Novel* (2011):

> One can say, for one thing, that the truth of novels cannot be rendered in any other form; it cannot be abstracted or codified, turned into thesis or proposition. Novelistic truth is not data, not reportage, not documentary, not philosophical tenet, not political slogan. Novelistic truth is dramatic, which means above all it has to do with character… In exploring character, the novel's key strength is the disclosure of human interiority. To the question, what does the novel do?, we might most pertinently answer: the novel does character, and the novel does interiority.

Character and interiority; no mention here of the novel's capacity not just to 'disclose' but to expand the remit of human experience, for instance, to offer temporary access to other ways of perceiving. Or of the novel as thought experiment, as a viable form of knowledge all of its own—let alone as a ticket to peak experience at the limits of language.

Recent energetic attempts to name and claim a successor to postmodernism persist in drawing upon a textbook version of literary history, at the expense of engaging fully with the realities of present-day literary practice, and with its neglected antecedents. Here, China Miéville's 'Five to Read' looks to those, past and present, who have failed to make the cut. Insofar as such a model ever could anywhere, the one that bisects the twentieth century more-or-less down the middle, dividing its paper assets between categories of modernism and postmodernism, has never comfortably applied here. On the whole, British writing embraced postmodern inclusivity for its capacity to welcome new voices, new perspectives—and, indeed, new market demographics—into the great tradition, but it tended to dispense with the formal and linguistic gym-nastics. Underwritten by an increasingly commercial book culture—subject to the bottom line of multinational publishing conglomerates and the vagaries of literary prizes—it quickly ossified into the set-in-stone author dynasties that continue to dominate accounts of British contemporary fiction.

In this Old Country, history has stubbornly refused to dissolve into textuality. Indeed, pressed to take a punt on tendencies, coteries or shared sensibilities amongst British fiction today, we might locate a likely successor to a postmodernism-that-wasn't in the hauntological, uncanny, or psycho-geographical inflections of novels by Will Self, A.L. Kennedy, Iain Sinclair, Ali Smith, Scarlett Thomas, Nicola Barker and David Peace. As one wag has commented, hauntology is, by now, so ubiquitous in Britain—in philosophy, music and the visual arts, as well as fiction—that it can be merely a fortnight away from having a newspaper column named after it. If you were looking for a fictional Britain, you could do much worse than Barker and Peace, who feature here in essays by Katy Shaw and Victor Sage. Barker's salty, Rabelaisian bizarrerie offers a truly democratic, and ordinarily strange, picture of Britain and the 'occult histories' of David Peace reflect a nation struggling to come to terms with the very worst of its recent past.

Perhaps at last, though, even academic critics, lumbered with their 'research' agendas, grant proposals, and the protocol of the new 'enterprise' university culture of 'business partnerships', 'knowledge transfer' and 'impact', are beginning to feel restless about institutional constraints on proper literary engagement. Despite Stewart Home's protestations to the contrary (in the essay printed here), we discern more generally and in the essays written by Maureen Freely, China Miéville, Andrew Crumey and in the interview with Jim Crace, a new desire to talk or at least whisper conspiratorially across the fence between the ivory tower and the shed at the bottom of the garden. Both the academic critic and the contemporary writer find themselves under threat and compromised—economically and existentially—by the re-structuring and re-development of the new globalised neo-Corporatisms, with their token nods to green recycling and New Age recovery, and their sinister and often systematic appropriations of everything from art to the social network to the 'event'. The work of art exists no longer in a Romantic-Modernist age of mechanical reproduction but in the disseminated and pervasive global networks of the neo-corporate and the new knowledge economy. Being 'local' is unavoidably a way of being 'global'; getting inside the singular consciousness may be less a business of flowing along a stream of consciousness than evoking a structure of feeling of a world that, as Musil discerned long ago, is filling up with men without qualities, men incorporated into the neo-corporate spaces of the new knowledge economy. If postmodernism was a lament for depths lost to late consumer capital, it was always easy prey to charges of mendacious and slippery complicity with the enemy. If we are currently now officially in an 'interregnum', past the post and into a new age of 're'—redevelopment, recycling, restructuring, reparation, reconciliation, residue, remainder, remembrance, recession—trying to rebuild foundations, recover roots and re-imagine a future re-connected with a revisioned past, we are also being forced to acknowledge how far past the post we are in other ways too—poised uncertainly but apocalyptically on the brink of environmental disaster and economic collapse. Artistically and imaginatively, though British and stranded on a sinking island, we too inhabit the new world of the globalised and the neo-corporate frozen style that deploys its resources in the professional management and production of the real. There is, quite discernibly, a new climate of seriousness, a sense of 'growing up' from postmodernism, but as fears of the death of the author abate that by no means presents new death-threats to the artistic imagination, to the comic, bizarre, dislocated, often eccentric, visionary, and above all *new* writing that we have tried to feature in the forthcoming pages of this special issue. Here we discern little or no yearning to crawl back under the comfort blanket of lyrical realism (whatever that is or was).

MAUREEN FREELY

The Strange Case of the Reader and the Invisible Hand

They may have set their sights too high, these two. But they have plenty of company. The Mediterranean village in which they are trying to live as cheaply as possible is packed with young writers who share their low opinion of conventional, commercial fiction, who dream of writing something some day that might stand alongside Beckett and Borges, Barth and Burroughs, and who joke, just a little nervously, that there's not much room left on that bookshelf, that all the best experiments have been done already, that if they wrote an entire novel in the shape of a gyre while standing on their head, they still wouldn't get much notice.

And almost every day there comes news of a new defection: X, who set out to be fiction's answer to Wittgenstein, has written a book with a plot. The thriller that Y wrote just to buy another year of freedom has sold to the movies, and so he's decided, what the hell? Why not buy a second year of freedom while the going's good? And so it goes, until summer turns to autumn and the cafes empty out, except for our two shivering aesthetes, who are more determined than ever that they will never, ever sell out.

They buy a charcoal brazier and struggle on through the winter, typing as fast as their half-frozen hands will allow. When spring is almost but not quite in the air, they run out of money, so they go to work for one of the village's wealthier expatriate artists, caring for his children and building his walls. Returning to their unheated cottage at dusk, they find themselves too exhausted to work. So they cut just one corner. They send off their works-in-progress, hoping that their editors will see enough in them to make a reasonable offer.

Their editors couldn't be more different from each other in personality and taste. But their responses are identical: 'we regret to tell you that there's no market for plotless prose, no matter how arresting its wordplay. The sad fact is that today's readers just won't stand for it. But, if, on the other hand . . . '

Worn down by their wealthy employers' walls and wailing children, our two shivering aesthetes decamp to the cafe to discuss that other hand.

You might have no patience for this precious pair. You might even say that they are best denuded of their arrogant illusions, that they should trying living in the real world for a while, if they hope ever to write anything worthwhile. You might add that even Hemingway had to do the real world thing, and that it was by doing battle with it that he found his voice. But when Hemingway sat drinking with Gertrude Stein discussing roses that were roses, when Robert Graves and Laura Riding stuck a pin in a map and discovered Deia, when Paul Bowles packed his bags for Morocco, and Cortazar headed for Paris, they, too, were preoccupied by money. They depended to a very large degree on wise friends with good taste and great fortunes. They also had editors who could afford to wait for the breakthrough book that could be ten years in the making. And they could count on an equally stable fraternity of reviewers, and on bookstores that were not chains. Not every author sold millions, but then again, not every author particularly wanted to. It was still an honourable thing to write fiction for a small and discriminating audience, and an aspiring writer could still make a small amount of money go a long way on a Mediterranean island, if she was better at budgeting than I was.

That was how things were in the mid 1970s, when I first began to write. Four decades on, the invisible hand of the free market has changed the game utterly. The global players that have swallowed up most of the grand old publishing firms must answer to their shareholders, who expect the same returns from books as they do from shoes. No one can wait ten years for a breakthrough book. Even in the small houses, founded for no other reason than to buck the trend, no one can afford *not* to listen to the sales and marketing departments, without whose blessing no book can go out into the world. That is not to say that the industry isn't full of secret idealists who manage against the odds to publish books they care about. And neither is it to overlook the signs that suggest audiences for literary fiction are larger and more diverse than ever. You might also wish to take heart from the rise and rise of literary festivals, unless you've worked for one. However artfully their directors might protest in their brochures, what they care about most, what they *have* to care about most, is bums on seats.

As for the internet: yes, so far, Amazon has been a plus for long-tail publishing, and so intermittently a plus for small literary houses, even if it's hurt both chain and independent bookstores mortally. And yes, some writers will do well out of electronic publishing. But it is thanks to the digital end of the neoliberal revolution that we have arrived at a moment when all the institutions that support and perpetuate literature are foundering—when copyright law is becoming increasingly irrelevant, when book pages are disappearing, along with the newspapers that once hosted them, when editors who actually edit mostly do so in their spare time, and imprints that were once proudly independent publishing houses get axed because they can't do 7% better year on year, and new writers must achieve the same instantly, or face publishing death.

What sort of phoenix rises from these ashes is anyone's guess. In my happy moments, I like to think that the neoliberal downturn will be a good thing for new and daring writers in the long run, if only because it will allow more room for innovation, and less room for the sorts of middle-aged gatekeepers who dominated the industry in the staid and solid 1970s. But while we're twisting in limbo, waiting to see what the Invisible Hand does next, it might be worth asking just how much the laws of the marketplace have shaped Anglophone writing over the past four decades.

This was not the question Mark McGurl set out to address in *The Program Era* (2009), his mischievous but rather brilliant account of the ways in which creative writing programmes shaped US post-war literary fiction. But the answer is there between the lines. Literary novelists took refuge in universities in increasing numbers after 1970 because they needed day jobs first and foremost, but also because their work had far greater value in university culture than it did in the increasingly cut-throat world of commercial publishing. Writers working in this rapidly expanding network of writing programmes did not just get a chance to nurture and shape new literary talents. They also served as patrons, publishing the best new fiction in their own magazines and university presses, connecting their brightest young things with the right mainstream editors, giving them the blurbs that encouraged the attention of the literary establishment, and (in due course) giving them jobs. McGurl traces one inevitable consequence of this informal system of support: the emergence of house styles, with some programmes favouring or even enforcing lean, character-based narratives, and just a few championing fictions too imaginative to fit into any box. What McGurl does not examine in much detail is what I witnessed during my own years of refuge in that network. Especially in remote areas (like El Paso, where I worked in the early 1980s, and Miami, where I worked next) writing programmes served as entry points for aspiring writers who came from backgrounds that made the New York based publishing industry seem more distant than the moon. Writing tutors were serving as talent scouts, and the better their discoveries did at the high-brow end of publishing, the more highly the industry rated the programmes in which they worked.

In Britain the story is different: with one very starry exception, universities did not go into the creative writing business until the 1990s, and it's only been over the past decade that we have begun to see the emergence of a national network. During the 1970s and 1980s, the best option for literary writers in the slow-sales bracket was to work (in-house or freelance) for the broadsheets, as they were then called, or for public broadcasting. This is how I made ends meet for about fifteen years from the late 1980s, and again I had plenty of company. The idea was to tread water until publishing a book that did well enough to make the day job redundant.

For many of my peers, if not for me, the dream came true. More often than not, their breakthroughs were hybrids that rewrote the conventions of nonfiction through the use of fiction techniques. Many touched on areas that their authors had stumbled upon as jobbing journalists—things they themselves would never have encountered had they managed to stay in those Mediterranean villages, mocking and refusing that Invisible Hand. What was original was their manner of writing: you could even argue that the most innovative writing produced during the last decades of the twentieth century in this country was in the realm of literary nonfiction. As someone who has written in this vein, I would of course like to agree. But I'd also want to point out that those of us who supported our families and our fiction habit by working in journalism during the last years of print pre-eminence were perhaps been over-shaped by the hands that fed us. The media deal in stock plots, after all. They operate a filtering system, whereby editors consciously or unconsciously seek to enforce political agendas, advertising categories, and social prejudices. While it is not too difficult to slip things through, and while there have always been areas of relative freedom in even the most politicised areas of the media, those of us who got ahead in this fractured world did so by listening oh-so-carefully to our editors' anxieties and prejudices, and we took those skills back into our work as writers of literary nonfiction and as novelists. Putting it crudely, we learned how to lose some in order to win some. And we won biggest when we dressed our literary wolves in the sort of sheep's clothing that agents and editors could sell.

Editors and agents were as mixed a bunch in the 1980s and 1990s as they are today. So let me confine my remarks to those whom my peers and I saw as being on our side. Even as our old publishing houses became imprints owned by conglomerates, answering to the norms and requirements of the market, there remained a significant number of editors and agents successful enough to run their own lists. But bit by bit their power was chipped away. Soon it was no longer enough for a division to make a profit overall, with a small number of big sellers subsidising the rest. It became more and more difficult for publishers to carry novelists for more than a book or two. If they didn't win prizes or sell in huge numbers, they were consigned to the dreaded 'midlist', the publishing industry's death row.

This is why so many of us were keen to take refuge in British universities as they began to see the point of creative writing programmes. Here, as in the US, these programmes have served as arks. Though everything we do in them is highly (and often stupidly) regulated, and though we, too, are guinea pigs in the great neoliberal experiment, British universities are nevertheless havens for literary writers. Like our scholarly colleagues, we perish if we don't publish. But at least we have salaries, and (for the moment at least) the quality of our work matters more than our sales figures. And when we go into the classroom, we don't have sales and marketing departments setting the rules for us. Though part of our job must be to equip our most promising students to do battle with the Invisible Hand, our first job is to educate them, both as readers and as writers. We do so by allowing them the sort of freedom we think all writers deserve, nurturing and guiding them as they mature, while also providing a point of entry for writers beyond the old boy networks that once dominated British publishing. As such we are serving not just as talent scouts. We are also keeping alive a literary tradition that the Invisible Hand would otherwise crush. You might wish to see us as invisible editors, looking after emerging writers until they are strong enough to hold their own.

I suspect I am like most university-based writers in having a limited commitment to my day job. I am not at all sure that I would have given quite as much time to teaching as I have done over the past fifteen years, had there not been the lure of that monthly pay check. But if I had to compile a list of the best writing I have encountered over just the past year, a great deal of it would consist of student work. I read most of it with a sinking heart, knowing that it does not fit into the selling categories. When I read work by a student who does actually have a chance in the cruel marketplace, my heart sinks, too. Because I know what will happen next: an agent, often a really good agent, will take this student on. There will follow a year of second, third and fourth drafts, as the writer and the agent work to turn the book into something commercially viable.

Even ten years ago, there was still a clear line to be drawn between the sort of guidance editors and agents gave a commercially motivated novelist and the sort they gave to novelists of a more literary persuasion. The line still exists, but it is blurring fast. How the Invisible Hand has crept into negotiations between literary writers and their editors is hard to chart. But let me give some sense of it by identifying one of the phantoms through which it makes its will felt.

This is the Reader, now a regular fixture in our conversations with even our most literary editors and agents. No one knows who the Reader is exactly, but everyone in the publishing industry knows it must be obeyed, or else. What the Reader wants most of all is a strong narrative, without which it will toss the book aside before the end of the first paragraph.

It's the Reader, incidentally, who keeps the amount of fiction published in English translation so very low. It's not translation in and of itself that the Reader mistrusts—just look at all the thrillers and mysteries or books masquerading as mysteries that do come out in translation, and do well. What the Reader won't stomach is that thing they still like in Europe and indeed just about everywhere in the world but here, not that we'd recognise it if we saw it, because the Reader banned it from the Anglophone world before you were born. This is the philosophical novel, in which speculation as well as wordplay count for more than plot. The Reader deems such books unreadable. It likes its ideas sugared, if at all.

I am using gender-neutral pronouns because the Reader's gender is uncertain. The Reader is a creature of a thousand veils, and with each veil, its desires change. When presented with a hard-edged thriller, it wants a murder on the first page, if not three murders. When presented with a psychological thriller with a female lead, that lead must be unmarried and 28 years old. If it's set in Asia, or Africa, or South America—anywhere hot and impoverished—it must be redolent with exotic sights, sounds, and smells, while racing along to a finish that confirms the Reader's worldview.

However, and in spite of the certainty of its pronouncements on any given day, the Reader's taste in strong narratives is inconstant. Basically, it wants a narrative that echoes whatever swept the prizes and the bestseller lists last year. This means that the wish list you hear about when you go in to negotiate contracts and revisions with your literary editor will in no way reflect the wishes of the Reader who picks up the finished copy. It will have tired of Dan Browns by then. It will have outgrown chick lit. It went to Addis Ababa last year and there was nothing but brown swirling dust.

If I were to write a history of publishing in this country over the past four decades, I would give most attention to the editors and agents who have fought the Invisible Hand and won, only to wake up the next morning to find that the rules of the game have changed yet again. And I would ask myself what I would do if I were in their shoes, if I'd been publishing one of life's great Originals, whose every book was more bizarre than the last, and somehow getting them past the philistines in sales—until the day arrived when the conglomerate that owned me decreed one day that every book I published must make a profit. I am quite sure that my next move would be to call in the Original, to steer her towards a novel with a strong narrative, just this once.

Here I should admit that I have always loved narrative—just as much as I love plotless wordplay and meandering philosophical speculation. I love fiction that electrifies me through its words or its invisible structures, fiction that makes me see the world as I have never seen it, if only for a few moments. That was what kept me reading as a child, and inspired me to study literature at university, and started me writing. For me the whole point of writing is to be free to think. If I wanted to live by narratives imposed on me by others, I would have gone into the church, or that modern place of worship, the trading floor.

And yet, to keep my hand in, I must still answer to the Reader. At the very least I must appear to meet its demands. And so that is the game I play, to keep my freedom as a writer, while also keeping myself solvent.

Here again, I have plenty of company. If I were to write a history of contemporary British fiction, that is the undercover rebellion I would seek to chart—the thousands of little ruses through which novelists working in Britain have challenged the narratives imposed on them, while seeming utterly docile on the surface. Like workers in satanic mills, perhaps. Or women before feminism. But just think how much more we could do, if we could cast off the Reader's chains.

PAUL CROSTHWAITE

'Soon the Economic System Will Crumble': Financial Crisis and Contemporary British Avant-Garde Writing

Since the mid-1980s, as Britain, or, more specifically, London, has emerged as a global financial centre rivalled only by New York the idioms, codes, and rituals of high finance have become pressing concerns for British novelists. These concerns became acutely urgent with the onset of the global financial crisis or 'credit crunch'. The sub-genre of contemporary British fiction dubbed 'crunch-lit' by the critic Sathnam Sanghera has achieved prominence, popularity, and acclaim in recent years, but the novels in question have so far proved wholly inadequate to their subject matter, attempting to impose the venerable fictional traditions of realism, personalisation, and moralisation onto a crisis that was in many ways unreal, impersonal, and amoral. In this essay, I suggest that for British fiction that fully acknowledges the intellectual and aesthetic challenges posed by financial crises we must look to earlier decades and to overtly avant-garde techniques: specifically to the experimental science fiction of Christine Brooke-Rose and the academic philosophy-cum-cyberpunk writing of Nick Land. Brooke-Rose's *Amalgamemnon* (1984) vividly imagines the impending catastrophic breakdown of a wholly computerised global financial system, from which human agents are excluded. Similarly, Land's 'theory-fictions' or, in his preferred term, 'hyperstitions' of the 1990s—most notably 'Meltdown' (1994)—construe the sprawling, anonymous circuits of contemporary financial capitalism as tending inexorably toward crisis. Both Brooke-Rose's and Land's texts overtly present themselves as prophecies of financial disaster; as such, their time has now arrived, eclipsing in importance and relevance more conventional texts that respond directly to the ongoing crises of financial capitalism.

When it Comes to the Crunch

The 'crunch-lit' novel that most fully exemplifies the failings of the form is also probably the best known and most widely celebrated example: Sebastian Faulks's *A Week in December* (2009), a panoramic portrayal of contemporary metropolitan life set in the early credit crunch days of December 2007. The attachment to realist conventions exhibited by this and similar novels is problematic because it results in a fundamental contradiction between content and form, since the phenomenon to which the text gives narrative shape, the phenomenon of contemporary financial crisis—abstract, cryptic, phantasmagoric—is everything that realism, with its air of transparency and emphasis on the material, the tangible, and the apprehensible, is not. *A Week in December*, like other credit crunch novels, places great emphasis on the unreality of financial exchange: such exchange is 'detached ... from the real world', 'semi-virtual', and 'magical[ly] self-sufficien[t]'.[1] Similarly, Justin Cartwright's *Other People's Money* (2011) describes advanced financial instruments as 'chimeras' and 'fables' that 'appear from nowhere' and then 'simply [implode]'.[2] The speculative, ontologically unstable condition that such texts attribute to finance capital would be conveyed to the reader with immeasurably greater power, however, if, rather than merely being described matter-of-factly, it were absorbed into the fabric of the narrative discourse itself.

In a further contradiction, works of crunch-lit typically maintain a realist style whilst depicting the dynamics of the credit crisis in profoundly counter-factual terms, by attributing this structural and systemic crisis of global finance capital to the actions of a small group of people, or even a single individual. A propensity familiar from the well-established sub-genre known as the financial thriller,[3] its clearest manifestation in novels responding to the credit crunch again appears in Faulks's *A Week in December*, whose protagonist, a hedge fund manager named John Veals, seeks to profit by single-handedly bringing down a thinly-veiled version of the Royal Bank of Scotland, and with it the wider British, and world, economies.

Hand in hand with credit crunch novels' tendency to personalise goes a propensity to moralise. In almost every example of the form, the roots of the crisis are ultimately found to lie in individuals' lamentable susceptibility to the age old sin of avarice. Faulks's John Veals, for example, '[cannot] be happy as a man if his positions [aren't] making money'.[4] Likewise, the protagonist of Alex Preston's *This Bleeding City* (2010), a Mayfair hedge fund manager, is persuaded to ignore the dangers of his trading activities by the prospect of buying 'a flat in Chelsea, a sports car, a huge television with speakers mounted high on the walls. I would live like those I envied, exist in their perfect world'.[5] The protagonist of Talitha Stevenson's *Disappear* (2010), meanwhile, regretfully comes to the realisation that her life with her hedge fund manager husband has been about nothing more than 'making money out of money and investing it in the fund again to make more money'.[6] To imagine a narrative in which, in contrast, the protagonists are not fully realised, psychologically complex, desirous individuals but rather anonymous, inhuman systems and networks may run contrary to the traditional inclinations of the novel, but it is a task demanded by the realities of contemporary finance capital and its periodic crises.

Figuring Crisis in Brooke-Rose and Land
The writings by Christine Brooke-Rose and Nick Land referred to above take on this challenge. As such, Brooke-Rose's *Amalgamemnon* and Land's 'Meltdown' (1994) and other, related texts exemplify the intellectual concerns and the challenges to formal convention that have distinguished the two writers' careers. *Amalgamemnon*'s focus on financial markets is typical of the interest in symbolic systems and structures that marks the experimental fiction written by the always-cosmopolitan Brooke-Rose (born to an English father and Swiss-American mother in Geneva, raised in Brussels, and educated in England) after she came under the influence of the French *nouveau roman* in the early 1960s, and especially after she left London in 1968 for a post at the radical new branch of the University of Paris at Vincennes. Similarly, the attention to the world of finance in 'Meltdown' and other pieces by Land is consistent with his sustained preoccupation with the most arcane and recondite dimensions of capitalist modernity. Land's growing desire to replicate the esoteric

qualities of futures trading, cybernetics, cryptology, chaos theory, and the burgeoning web culture of the 1990s in the style and form of his own writing, however, increasingly led him into conflict with the disciplinary and institutional norms that, as a lecturer in Philosophy at the University of Warwick, he was expected to think and write within. Having resigned from Warwick and abandoned academia in 1998, Land is now based in one of the frontier zones of the new global capitalist order, Shanghai, from where he continues to issue gnomic online dispatches on urbanism, economics, and technology.[7]

There are striking similarities between the visions of financial upheaval offered by *Amalgamemnon* and those which appear in 'Meltdown' and the other texts that cluster around it in Land's oeuvre. Brooke-Rose's novel centres around the musings of a soon-to-be-redundant humanities professor as she reads Herodotus, listens to the radio, imagines herself and her acquaintances in scenarios drawn from classical myth, and contemplates the end of the world. Financial and economic crises loom large in the text's prognostications of impending cataclysm. 'Soon', we are told in the opening pages, 'the economic system will crumble'.[8] For the sake of 'mounting profits', the 'rich countries' are burdening 'those of the third world' with debt, endangering 'the world's whole banking system which in its collapse would plunge the people of all nations but especially the poor into the deepest misery' (73). The text ponders, too, the uncertain and potentially destabilising consequences of a shift in the locus of global economic hegemony toward East Asia, a shift already discernible in the early 1980s as the liberalisation of the Chinese economy, in particular, began to take effect: 'The people of the Pacific, with their strong business sense their willingness to work their nimble electronic fingers will cause the centre of wealth in the twentyfirst century to shift from one ocean to another. Both Atlantic capitalism and Asian State capitalism may crumble from inside' (69-70).

'Meltdown' is, if anything, still more apocalyptic. Its tone of chaos and collapse epitomises the style of the 'hyperstitions'—'fictional quantities' or 'semiotic productions' that 'make themselves real'[9]—which Land produced in the 1990s, in which continental philosophy (primarily the work of Gilles

Deleuze and Félix Guattari) merges with a cyberpunk landscape reminiscent of William Gibson's *Sprawl* trilogy. 'Meltdown' presents the capitalist epoch inaugurated by the 'commoditization take-off' (441) of Europe half a millennium ago as an age of perpetual, self-generating crisis that is now approaching a state of maximum disorder or total 'deterritorialisation'. Marked by a 'terminal speculative bubble crisis' (442), this chaotic contemporary condition is also, as in *Amalgamemnon*, distinguished by a new disequilibrium in world markets and a breakdown of the financial and economic power of the West: 'As sino-pacific boom and automatized global economic integration crashes the neocolonial world system, the metropolis is forced to re-endogenize its crisis. Hyper-fluid capital deterritorializing to the planetary level divests the first world of geographic privilege' (449).

In contrast to the 'crunch-lit' novels of recent years, *Amalgamemnon* and 'Meltdown' distance themselves from the norms of realist fiction in ways that resonate with the financial processes they describe. Not only does *Amalgamemnon* favour unfettered speculation about the world's potential fate over a verisimilar depiction of its actual historical condition, it refuses to project a 'world' at all in the sense of an internally consistent fictional domain in which characters, objects, and events are clearly delineated and arrayed in space and time. On the contrary, there are few indications as to which portions of the text are spoken by the professor-protagonist, which by other characters, and which by some voice entirely lacking any 'bodily' instantiation, nor where the line is to be drawn between words that make up an internal monologue and those spoken out loud. Moreover, as Steven Connor comments, 'the restriction of the novel to non-realized verbal forms, which is to say, principally future and conditional tenses and imperative and subjunctive moods … means that it is very hard to distinguish what actually happens … from what is surmised, desired, or imagined'.[10] As Brian McHale notes, 'the entire world of *Amalgamemnon*—its narrator, character, events, time and space, etc.—dangles in ontological limbo'.[11] The novel, then, registers in its very form what the likes of Faulks and Cartwright are content merely to describe. Like finance capital itself, Brooke-Rose's narrative is a speculative, hypothetical, imaginative realm, cut adrift from the material conditions of daily life and shot through with uncertainty as to whether it is in any sense 'real'.

'Meltdown' is similarly anti-realist, both in the simple sense of being *unrealistic*—of describing a world that is a wildly imaginative extrapolation of logics immanent within our own—and in the more subtle and significant sense of challenging realism's conventional modes of address. Where the language of realism is typically spare, direct, and measured, the better to convey an illusion of transparency, Land's discourse in 'Meltdown' and similar texts wilfully blends extreme abstraction—through the use of technical vocabularies drawn from fields such as philosophy, psychoanalysis, economics, cybernetics, mathematics, biology, and complexity theory—with a manic, delirious style of delivery. Again, Land's writing thus appears as the precise textual correlate of contemporary finance capital, a system as abstract and technical as it is dynamic and unstable.

If, to borrow terms from the French theorist Jean-Joseph Goux, the 'representative' or 'truthful' realism of Faulks and the other crunch-lit novelists aspires nostalgically to the condition of a 'gold-language', in and through which 'the real would be conveyed without mediation', then the 'aesthetic based on nonfiguration or abstraction' practiced by Brooke-Rose and Land registers the fact that its subject matter is 'a type of economic circulation in which money is reduced to a "token" that lacks any intrinsic value and whose *convertibility* is increasingly hypothetical'.[12] In her critical study, *A ZBC of Ezra Pound* (1971), Brooke-Rose mentions the 'synthesis between money and language as corruptible exchange, which is now occupying … the young Marxist critics and semiologists of the *Tel Quel* group', of whom Goux was one of the leading figures.[13] In a confirmation of this 'synthesis', *Amalgamemnon* not only enacts, but also expressly depicts, a crisis in the relationship between signs and 'denotata' (real, existing objects of reference) which is as much monetary as it is linguistic:

> Professor Albireo Cygnus will lecture tomorrow in a big hall and
> deny the rumours that the sign could be about to collapse, although
> any one system possessing, from a pragmatic point of view, great

modeling power, may in a latter phase come to seem a set of signs without denotata . . .

> [A]s for what will happen next the semiotic system will crash the wall streets of the cities will swarm with the dark passions and black panics of small savers high gamblers and tall banktellers of tales. (78)

Amalgamemnon parodies the tendency, typical of works of crunch-lit, to personalise financial crises by depicting a figure who, as Debra Malina suggests, appears to be none other than 'capitalism it/herself'.[14] Brooke-Rose highlights the inadequacy of responses to crisis that think purely in terms of individual desire and action by emphasising precisely the *im*personality of this notional 'person'. The student revolutionaries who kidnap this strange entity know that 'she' will die 'unless fed exclusively on capital' (81) and attempt a radical reprogramming operation, feeding her not with infusions of capital but with readings from *Das Kapital* (84). In one of the novel's strangest and most suggestive moments, the resistance that this strategy encounters is conveyed via what can only be described as the direct interior monologue of an entity entirely bereft of interiority, and of centre, essence, consistency, and coherence:

> I could take vaster risks within the mind construct of high finance and the perpetual excitement of the movement of capital. They'll never understand that they can't win ... as long as I continue to calculate myself into existence out of imaginary sums, increasing myself per day per minute if necessary, after all every financial operation might be pure fiction from my point of view. (106)

In a similar way, it is clear that the volatility in the capitalist system charted in Land's 'Meltdown' occurs not at the instigation of some tyrannical financial titan—one of the John Veals of this world—but rather in accordance with the purely formal 'axiomatic' through which 'machine-code-capital recycles itself' (445). As an impersonal system of networks, structures, and protocols, irreducible to the individuals who populate or enact them, finance capital, for Brooke-Rose and Land, is incompatible with moralising critique. As Land makes clear in 'Machinic Desire' (1993), not only is "greed" merely a psychologistic means of characterising the 'profit-seeking tropism of ... transnational capitalism', but human desire is on the verge of being entirely excluded from the system, as financial exchange is delegated more and more to computerised trading systems—or 'silicon viro-finance automatisms'—programmed to pursue their own indifferent course (337).[15]

It is this kind of vision of financial markets that marks out Land's and Brooke-Rose's texts as in many ways more compelling fictional guides to the contemporary credit crisis than the cluster of novels directly spawned by the crash. The powerful contemporary resonances of *Amalgamemnon* and 'Meltdown' are heightened, moreover, by the ways in which they consciously project themselves beyond their own immediate historical moments, into future scenarios in which their dire economic prophecies will be realised. Prophecy is a particular preoccupation in *Amalgamemnon*. Most notably, the narrative's status as a 'syntactic lipogram',[16] in which all but the dialogue passages maintain the future tense, conveys a sense that the events described must inevitably occur at some indeterminable future point. As Brooke-Rose noted in an interview given two months after the Black Monday stock market crash of October 1987, the catastrophic anticipations of the novel would be realised all too soon:

> For forty years the economists have been telling us, 'Oh no, there couldn't possibly be another stock market crash like 1929.' Well, maybe technically the crash of 1987 wasn't like 1929, but I'd been waiting for it and I know nothing about finance. So this is what I was trying to explore, why it is we are led by people who can't predict what it's their job to predict.[17]

Narrated in the present tense, with all its urgency and immediacy, 'Meltdown' ostensibly tells us what *is* happening, whilst also, like *Amalgamemnon*, implicitly identifying itself as a projection of what *will* happen. Land's text is similarly self-conscious about its proleptic orientation, tracing a historical trajectory that—like the Mesoamerican Long Count calendar in the imaginations of New Age mystics—appears to zero in on the year 2012: 'Converging upon terrestrial meltdown singularity, phase-out culture accelerates through its digitech-heated adaptive landscape, passing through compression thresholds normed to an intensive logistic curve: 1500, 1756, 1884, 1948, 1980, 1996, 2004, 2008, 2010, 2011 . . . ' (443). As Land explains, these dates chart modernity's race 'through intensive half-lives'.[18] Though the years enumerated after 1500 (which presumably stands as modernity's symbolic start date) are at least partly the arbitrary products of a numerical scheme in which the gaps between the integers must progressively halve, it is a confirmation of Land's underlying claim about the intensification of technological, economic, and political processes that each year carries some iconic world-historical resonance: the beginning of the Seven Years' War; the International Meridian and Berlin conferences; the Berlin Blockade; the Reagan election; Kasparov and Deep Blue; the Madrid bombings . . . Speaking in the late 1990s, one of Land's former colleagues wryly recalled how Land went through a 'glorious phase in which he offered millennial prophecies for the next global meltdown in world markets, a deduction based on past such cycles. It rather smacked of an infatuation with the power of numbers'.[19] The tone here is affectionately mocking, but looking now at the version of these numerological musings committed to print in 'Meltdown', one cannot help but notice that, whether coincidently or not, Land's countdown includes the year—2008—which saw undoubtedly the most severe financial crisis since 1929, and arguably the worst in history. As the aftershocks of that crisis rumble on, the stark final paragraph of 'Meltdown' seems more ominous than ever: 'To be continued.'

NOTES

I am grateful to fellow panellists and members of the audience at the 'First Fictions' festival hosted by the University of Sussex in January 2012—especially Peter Boxall, Bryan Cheyette, David James, Andrew Pepper, and Katy Shaw—for their helpful responses to an earlier version of this article.
[1] Sebastian Faulks, *A Week in December* (London: Hutchinson, 2009), 102-03.

[2] Justin Cartwright, *Other People's Money* (London: Bloomsbury, 2011), 80, 71, 103.

[3] On financial thrillers, see Nicky Marsh, *Money, Speculation, and Finance in Contemporary British Fiction* (London: Continuum, 2007), ch. 4; and my 'Blood on the Trading Floor: Waste, Sacrifice, and Death in Financial Crises', *Angelaki* 15.2 (2010), 3-17.

[4] Faulks, *A Week in December*, 14.

[5] Alex Preston, *This Bleeding City* (London: Faber and Faber, 2010), 117.

[6] Talitha Stevenson, *Disappear* (London: Virago, 2010), 214.

[7] An anthology of Land's work, *Fanged Noumena: Collected Writings*, 1987-2007, edited by Robin Mackay and Ray Brassier, was published in 2011 (Falmouth, UK: Urbanomic; New York: Sequence).

[8] Christine Brooke-Rose, *Amalgamemnon* (Manchester: Carcanet, 1984), 7; hereafter cited parenthetically.

[9] Land, 'Occultures' (1999), 'Origins of the Cthulhu Club' (c. 1998-1999), *Fanged Noumena*, 552, 579; texts from *Fanged Noumena* hereafter cited parenthetically.

[10] Steven Connor, *The English Novel in History, 1950-1995* (London: Routledge, 1996), 40.

[11] Brian McHale, "'I draw the line as a rule between one solar system and another": The Postmodernism(s) of Christine Brooke-Rose', in *Utterly Other Discourse: The Texts of Christine Brooke-Rose*, ed. Ellen G. Friedman and Richard Martin (Normal, IL: Dalkey Archive Press, 1995), 202.

[12] Jean-Joseph Goux, *The Coiners of Language*, trans. Jennifer Curtiss Gage (Norman: University of Oklahoma Press, 1994), 93, 92, 17, 93; italics in original.

[13] Christine Brooke-Rose, *A ZBC of Ezra Pound* (Berkeley and Los Angeles: University of California Press, 1971), 235-36.

[14] Debra Malina, *Breaking the Frame: Metalepsis and the Construction of the Subject* (Columbus: Ohio State University Press, 2002), 83.

[15] For an extended theorisation of the 'automatism' of financial crises (partly informed by Land's work), see my 'Is a Financial Crisis a Trauma?', *Cultural Critique* (forthcoming).

[16] Jean-Jacques Lecercle, 'Reading Amalgamemnon', in *Utterly Other Discourse*, 155.

[17] Ellen G. Friedman and Miriam Fuchs, 'A Conversation with Christine Brooke-Rose', in *Utterly Other Discourse*, 35.

[18] Qtd. in Charles J. Stivale, *The Two-Fold Thought of Deleuze and Guattari: Intersections and Animations* (New York: Guilford Press, 1998), 92.

[19] Qtd. in Simon Reynolds, 'Renegade Academia', http://energyflashbysimonreynolds. blogspot.com/2009/11/renegade-academia-cybernetic-culture.html.

JENNIFER HODGSON

An Interview with Jim Crace

Jim Crace has just had a very close shave. 'This time last year I abandoned a book. I'd sold it in America and in Britain, I'd spent the money, they'd want the money back. We'd lose the house. It was a really, really serious situation,' he remembers. 'You always think, don't lose your nerve, persevere . . . And in the past it's always worked.' This time it didn't. 'I thought I'd lost my mojo. I thought, "I've got a copy date, I've got to deliver a book at Christmas. I haven't got a book to write." I was in deep shit. That was on the Tuesday. I started *Harvest* on the Friday.' He mimes wiping sweat from his brow. 'So I wrote that book in six months and I delivered it on the same day that I should have delivered the old one. *Bloody hell*, I thought, *that was a narrow escape*. I felt like some kid in a boy's comic: "Phew! That was a close one."'

In May, when we meet, sweating discreetly in the long garden of his Birmingham home on the hottest day of the year, he's still in what he describes as 'the bruised aftermath'. *Harvest* (due out in early 2013), is set in a feudal community during the farm enclosures that did away with traditional rights to common land. The novel is, as with almost all of his others, historically and geographically nonspecific. People can't resist attempting to locate Crace (although it misses the point entirely); my hunch is Tudor-era and English. He is back in familiar unfamiliar territory here, after a sojourn in the (not quite) real world with his 2010 jazz novel, *All That Follows*.

This next book will be his last. 'I've written eleven novels and that's plenty. I know that the inevitable end of a career in writing is bitterness. You've written so many and people aren't paying attention to you any longer. So I want to get out before that kicks in'. Although he's still smarting, he thinks he'll try drama next: 'Big, blousy, highly-dramatised, National-Theatre-type things. Not Stoppardian dialogue-driven pieces, but spectacle-driven pieces . . . I want to try my hand at something more collaborative. Writing for the theatre, I'd have colleagues. All I see is people like you once in a while, and that's no good.'

Crace would rather not pontificate about his art of fiction. On much of what we talk about when we talk about writing—influences, inspiration, practice and (especially this last one) autobiographical resonance—he flatly but amiably will not be drawn. He'll talk at length about anything and everything, but when it comes to the writing life, he tends to rely on his patter. He apologises if I've heard it before.

Typically ingenuous, he describes what he does like this: 'I embark on this thing and hope I'm going to lose my way and that what takes over and what becomes the guide of the book will somehow be good.' When I venture my own take on *Harvest*, he thanks me; tells me, 'that's very useful'. I think, for a moment, that he's being sarcastic. He's not. He can be, he assures me, but he's not here. 'I very often don't know what I've got on my hands', he admits, 'I can't really describe it until I read the critics, then I'll have a spiel, and then I'll be able to read it in public'.

Crace, famously, doesn't do research. He claims no kith or kin amongst the great and the good of the British novel. 'Never knew anybody, never wanted any part of that', he says, 'I prefer to hang out with jazzmen'. Nowadays he reads non-fiction. And it should come as no surprise to readers familiar with the fictional milieu Adam Begley neatly christened "Craceland" that he is a keen natural historian who, generally, would much rather be walking, caving or twitching than writing novels.

His books have a kind of autonomous existence; Crace maintains that there are elements of his novels that he cannot account for. The occultish grammar of objects—beetles, stones, cracks in wood—by which his disparate oeuvre hangs together, for instance. 'My books are very schematic. It's almost as if the novels themselves have decided there will be running threads through. I really couldn't explain except that the books want them'. He recently discovered that he has a fictional kink: 'Why do so many women get their heads shaved in my books? I don't know where it's come from, or what it means'. It might be the product of reading Hemingway's *For Whom the Bell Tolls* as a teenager, he thinks, or perhaps of taking a fancy to Jean Seberg in *Saint Joan* and *Breathless* around the same time. 'But that's only me trying to make sense of why my books do that.'

'None of that is being cute', Crace insists, 'why would you want to spend so much time alone in the house staring at the screen—with your neighbours avoiding you because you're the mad writer—if it didn't provide you with some kind of magic and some kind of awe. Now, this sounds funny but I think that's why I love writing novels, and why I've chosen not to research my novels, to leave them entirely to the imagination. Because I find what the imagination provides so thrilling.'

Critics suspect that all this is strategic obfuscation. That Crace is being tricksy. That he's cunningly guarding both his own privacy and that of his strange and beguiling novels by constructing this laconic and maddeningly matter-of-fact public persona. They're fascinated, belabouringly so, by the contrast between the uneven, uneasy modernity of the unnamed hinterlands that provide the settings for his books, and his quiet, conventional (or mundane, as the ever-self-effacing Crace would have it) life in the arty suburbs of Britain's second city. Like J.G. Ballard, curtain-twitching on suburban psychosis in Shepperton, they're convinced that Crace, too, must be up to something.

As a nation of readers, Brigid Brophy characterised the British as ill-at-ease and bashful about the fictiveness of their fictions, equating stories with daydreaming and daydreaming with masturbation, and believing both to be bad for the eyesight. Perhaps it's this puritanical streak that accounts for our mistrust of this arch fabulator. *The Devil's Larder* (2001) is composed of sixty-four slices of bizarrerie that riff upon Britain's changing relationship with food and consumption in terms carnal and grotesque and of manners and mores. Reviewers were perplexed to note that Crace's recipes were not intended to be followed. One food writer took particular umbrage at his suggestion as to what one might do with an aubergine. They were astounded, he recalls, that he had 'simply made it up'.

Crace doesn't understand what all the fuss is about. 'This business of simply making stuff up is with what the traditions of literature are concerned. There's no such thing as a Minotaur, they've simply made it up. Simply making it up is an ancient tradition, more ancient than the conventions we labour under now', he explains. If happy families are all alike then who would want to read a fiction drawn from his? 'I'm baffled by what the critics say. It's not like I'm ducking and diving. It's just the way things are. You wouldn't want to read the story of my life because it's too smug, it's too lucky. Literature prefers divorce to long marriages, it prefers ill health to good health, it prefers war to peace'.

In 2005, *The Scotsman* made reference to Crace as 'the cult American writer'. There is some accuracy in their misnomer. Perhaps he sits rather more comfortably in the yarn-spinning tradition of Barth, Pynchon and Gass than in our own more sensible, empirical one. The non-places of late modernity that the novels inhabit might just as well be Sydney as Singapore as Sacramento. But the short story with which he made his name as a writer of fiction, 'Annie, California Plates', with its hep talk and hitchhiking, is pure Americana, an out-and-out homage to the Beat Generation Crace admired.

Certainly, he admits, he enjoys a higher standing amongst readers and critics on the other side of the Atlantic. He was awarded the National Book Critics Circle Fiction Award in 1999 for *Being Dead*; in 1992, the E.M. Forster Award from the American Academy of Arts; and the GAP International Prize for Literature for *The Gift of Stones* in 1989. He's taken on what he describes as a cushy gig teaching creative writing at the University of Texas at Austin. 'The idea of going to Texas just seemed sexy and interesting . . . And it's not really teaching is it? It's half an afternoon a week chatting to talented novelists.' Incidentally, he's wholly in favour of the enterprise: 'I think there's something very elitist about denying that writing can be learned or at least that your skills can be honed.'

Still, at the end of a twenty-six-year, eleven-novel career in fiction, Crace's writing life remains mysterious, apparently even to him. He's a nine-to-five only writer; no burning of the midnight oil for him, he likes real life too much.

But he claims what happens when he sits at his desk is, more or less, out of his hands. He calls it a 'form of abandonment' to a narrative impulse that is, he maintains, 'hardwired' into all of us. When pressed, he'll claim a fluke genesis. His new novel, for example, is product of happenstance: the ridge-and-furrow fields of the English countryside he's always loved, and an exhibition of sixteenth century watercolour landscapes he happened to attend.

In an article published that week in the *Guardian*, Jonathan Franzen addresses those perennial questions asked of novelists: 'Who are your inspirations?', for instance, 'Is your fiction autobiographical?' Franzen, citing no less than Nabokov as his authority, contests the idea that fiction has the ability to "take over", to usurp the authority of its author. 'I catch a whiff of self-aggrandisement', he writes, 'the notion presupposes a loss of authorial will, an abdication of intent. The novelist's primary responsibility is to create meaning, and if you could somehow leave this job to your characters you would necessarily be avoiding it yourself.'[1] Crace thinks all this is a bit rich, coming from Franzen: 'Perhaps it's true of him, but it's not true of me. There really is an abandonment. There really is the belief that because fictional narrative is ancient it's learnt a lot. It knows a lot, it's wise and it's generous and not to abandon yourself to that is a kind of arrogance as well. It's a real friend to you.'

It's 'not a New Age thing', he's quick to add, though at times it certainly sounds like one. On the contrary, it's thoroughly and sensibly Darwinian: 'All writers are doing is doing something formally, between hard covers, that all of us do informally as a necessary function of being human beings. We keep on imagining the future and reinventing the past . . . it's a necessary function of human consciousness, to be a narrative person.' Narrative, for Crace, is an evolutionary adaptation, 'if it were not we wouldn't still be storytellers', he insists. 'People would be happier, and more sociable, and more attractive to the opposite sex, and have better relationships if only they could be more narrative . . . It's how you get the girlfriend, it's how you get the boyfriend, it's being able to talk in pubs.'

The theory of narrative to which Crace subscribes—the idea the humans construct their own identities by writing and rewriting the stories of their experience—has, in recent decades, become fashionable, ubiquitous even, amongst fields as various as psychology, theology, sociology, philosophy, politics, medicine and indeed even finance. 'We are all virtuoso novelists', as cognitive scientist and philosopher, Dan Dennett, puts it, we 'try to make all our material cohere into a single good story . . . that story is our autobiography' and the 'chief fictional character . . . of that autobiography is one's self.'[2] It is generally assumed that we self-tellers are, most of us, instinctive Realists; concerned with fidelity and veracity, with reason and probability. We might fib, exaggerate, misremember or gloss the detail but we do so in service of the unity and coherence of our own story.

For Crace, however, our narrative adaptation might just as equally be given to falsification, to confabulation, to all-out lies. He insists that to be a narrative person is not simply to make the fragments of contingent experience cohere, to graft on a beginning, middle and an ending. 'The oil of the human imagination is fantastic', he insists. 'The person who won't embroider is the bore. The bullshit artist is the person we adore, as long as he doesn't do any harm'.

The idea that we are all, by our very nature, tall-tale-tellers has proved rather troublesome for those proponents of the idea that crafting an autobiographical narrative is the key to the good life. Certainly, Crace is well aware that people are ill-at-ease with lies. 'The kind of lying I do and always did was never to deceive you. It was to be amusing and entertaining and generous', he assures. 'By nature I'm a liar. I was always a fibber. When I was a kid I would always tell stories. I could never understand why people didn't like me telling stories. I thought that to take a little anecdote that happened and to add a few extra details was a generous act. I still don't get why it isn't.'

It is problematic, too, for literary critics, for whom this imaginative function is what makes *literary* narrative unique and valuable. I don't think his insistence that we all share this capacity for fiction is just Cracian modesty. It's an ethical thing, a bottom-up optimism about the world. And it's political too. He's deeply ambivalent about a British literary intelligentsia that he suggests—with apologies for being 'a terrible Marxist'—remains peopled with 'Oxbridge, white, heterosexual males'.

Crace comes clean: 'I've got a class thing, you see. It's ridiculous but I do believe in the class system, I do believe in class warfare, I do believe it's a big issue.' He is one of an increasingly lesser-spotted breed of Old Lefty; weaned on the (old) Labour Party, on trade unionism and social justice by his political activist, autodidact father. 'I sound like a terrible Marxist, a Stalinist'—that caveat again—'but I cling to things. I love my dad and I cling to the things that were important to him. That's not a very good reason, that's not a very intellectual reason for hanging onto prejudices, but it's a good emotional one.'

He was a big reader as an earnest young man, of both the muscular, political novelists like Steinbeck, Tressell and Orwell that were deemed (almost) acceptable on the North London council estate where he grew up, and the Beat writers that weren't. 'I was a little squirt. If I'd come back talking about Jack Kerouac and Walt Whitman I'd have got a punch', he recalls. 'But politics and trade unionism and journalism were sort of acceptable and I think that was part of the inheritance I got from my dad. That that's what I ought to do, if I was going to be a writer.'

Crace began his career as the "pet Lefty" at two British newspapers not exactly known for their progressive bias, *The Daily Telegraph* and *The Sunday Times*. 'I had integrity, I hope, and I was reliable but I wasn't a big writer, I was never going to make big waves as a journalist', he says. 'Now this sounds very po-faced—I'm quite puritanical actually, as well as not being very puritanical—but when I was a journalist, I would never tell a single lie. I wasn't puritanical about the truth because I thought that the truth had to be adhered to but it wouldn't serve your purposes. I always believed that the truth provides socialism. If you tell the absolute truth about circumstances, the truth is left-wing, I think.'

In the end, it was this integrity that precipitated his departure from journalism. In the mid-eighties, Crace was sent to report on the Broadwater Farm estate in North London, a year after the Tottenham Riots. The paper already had its angle: Broadwater was a "hellhole estate", sunk in racial tensions, mob violence and social problems, and on the brink of revenge riots. He found the estate wasn't such a hellhole after all. 'I'm from North London, and I know to call somewhere a "hellhole of an estate" is nonsense. It was a working-class estate, full of very good people who weren't earning much.' Crace had found his own angle: 'It wasn't a hellhole! It was a scoop, a bloody scoop!' The feature—all 7000 words of it—was pulled the day before the issue went to press. 'So I walked away from journalism and that was it', he recalls. Crace downplays the heroics of the gesture: 'I had to be principled. Fortunately, I had just sold *Continent* for a lot of money in the States, so I could afford to be principled.'

Although he migrated with ease from puritanical truth to not-so-puritanical lies, it's clear that Crace is a somewhat reluctant storyteller. Always an inveterate yarn-spinner—'I was great to smoke dope with', he tells me—Crace 'never intended to become a writer of fiction. I was a lover of fiction, but it seemed bourgeois to me and still does. Particularly the kind of writing I've ended up doing', he admits. 'I think that the puritanical side of me, if I'd even imagined aged seventeen the kind of writing I would do in the future, it would have been leafleteering. It would have been banner-waving writing, in which the politics were not timid or obscure, in which the message was quite clear. Whereas in the kind of writing I've ended up doing, it's clear there's politics in there, but my books aren't placards. If anything they don't close down on a slogan, they open out.'

His first book, abandoned before *Continent* (1986), his debut proper, was an attempt at such a novel. It was about personal politics, Crace's response to living through the "radical" seventies; a decade when, he suggests, so much of what purported to be political was actually about making the "right" lifestyle choice. 'My wife is a feminist, of course, and I'm a fellow traveller. One of the things that we didn't like about the feminist movement was that it was all about "getting my shit together". And of course that's important, but it can't exclude the other things.' The novel did not come easily, however: 'I didn't know what the next word was going to be, let alone the next chapter, or how it was going to end. It was like pushing a huge boulder up a very steep hill every day.'

Then he was asked to review Gabriel García Márquez's *In Evil Hour*. 'I remember thinking, *I can do that. I can do that in my sleep!* And I started *Continent*. And I felt at home. I wasn't being a puritanical journalist; I was just making stuff up—making up whole continents, making up languages, making up wildlife, inventing plants. That's the mischievous side of me. I make the real seem unlikely, and the unlikely seem so convincing that you swallow it. That's the trick I like to play.'

Even now, Crace seems to regret that he didn't turn out to be a Steinbeck, an Orwell or a Tressell. He thinks his own novels tend to preach to the choir: 'I'm not talking to people that don't basically share the same attitudes as me', he says. 'I think that if you're a political person and if you want to contribute to agendas, then writing my kind of fiction is a waste of time . . . I know how my readers vote and I know their relationship to red meats. Basically, left-wing vegetarians of a certain age and attitude read my books.' He often finds that his books don't reflect his politics: 'In many respects, my books are more reactionary than I am . . . If you allow the moment of abandonment to happen in principle, then you have to accept that it's a real thing. The book can, very often, have an opinion of its own that won't match yours.'

Continent, for instance, catches a neither-here-nor-there but startlingly familiar realm at the flashpoint of transition. Its seven stories are preoccupied with the struggle to reconcile the inheritance of a rural past that is felt to be more authentic and more cohesive, and yet stunted by quackery and superstition, with an encroaching modernity which promises an ambivalent sort of progress. '*Continent* always takes the side of the old ways of humankind rather than the new ways', he says. This "small c" conservatism is something intrinsic to the novel form for Crace: 'Fiction tends to do that, fiction always prefers to wise old man to the come-uppity young man.'

Crace's 1997 novel, *Quarantine*, a reimagining of the temptation of Christ, gained him an unlikely following (and one or two enemies) amongst America's Christian Right. 'It's a much more religious book that you'd expect from a North Korean-style atheist as I am', he says. 'I went on a Southern Baptist radio show, and because I was a white, middle-class, chirpy chappy they were saying, "Jim, if I could get you back, Martha would cook you up some grits and we'd soon have you down in your own church home and you'd be a fuller human being, believe me, Jim'", he recalls. What raised hackles most, incidentally, was the novel's uncapitalised "god": 'I used to get a letter once a month from America that would say, "Dear jim crace, now how do you like it, calling our saviour, the dear lord, 'god'?" He thought this was really punishing me', Crace recalls. He didn't keep this religious fanbase. I doubt very much that they were fooled by the retitling of his 2003 novel of sex and citizenship, *Six*, as *Genesis* in America. They would be long gone, after the wholly non-redemptive depiction of the afterlife in 1999's *Being Dead*.

'If I'd written *Quarantine* from my own viewpoint, it would have been an in-your-face, no-time-for-you, insulting-all-religions book. But what was interesting to me was that it wasn't.' If the fictions are more reactionary than their author, they are also less dogmatic, less sure of themselves—'less bigoted', as he puts it. 'I wish I'd written those big, sloganeering novels that changed the hearts and minds of men and women—and there are novels that do that. Nevertheless, there's something else that novels do that also matters. And that is to undermine thinking, to send you away. I hope the debate begins when you reach the last page of my novels.' Narrative's tightrope walk between the fictional and the empirical—its equivocation, its dissonance, its hybridity— 'reveals a whole raft of ambiguities and raises questions.' He continues: 'I think that the different kind of truth you find in fiction is also left-wing by nature, that's what I feel. Narrative's impulses are left-wing, is what I think.'

I hazard an attempt to pin Crace down: Am I right in detecting the influence of another old Lefty, E. P. Thompson, in his novels? He, slippery as a fish, thinks he might have come across the British historian and socialist in his younger, more puritanical days. Then is he too attempting to 'rescue' his protagonists from what Thompson called the 'enormous condescension of posterity'? 'It's true. In my books existing narratives are confronted . . . Each of my books takes an existing narrative and tries to set the record straight . . . Working class people are not without blemish, but I try to make them the heroes and heroines, rather than the old heroes and heroines of history', he says. 'One of the narratives about women that I hope my books confront is the Hollywood narrative that if you see a good-looking woman with flowing locks and a large bosom, she's the heroine. And not only is she the heroine, but good things are going to happen to her, virtue will adhere to her. And of course that's a lie: *abandon all hope everyone else in the world that is not without blemish and is not entirely virtuous . . .* The women in my books, I hope, are not seen as good-looking, because that's a sort of irrelevancy, they're seen as strong.'

Quite the opposite is true of Crace's men, however. In *Arcadia*, protagonist Rook is described as a 'firebrand turned to ashes'; such a description might apply across the board. The men of Craceland are reluctant protagonists, let alone heroes. Crace's plots frequently draw to a dénouement that calls for direct action; the men dither, they flap, they defer. They leave when they'd rather stay (*Harvest*), they stay when they want to leave (*The Pesthouse*). *All That Follows*'s jazz saxophonist, Lennie Lessing, is on sabbatical—and not only from music. This former political activist has, as his wife, Francine, taunts him: 'gone decaf'. He pads around in a kind of domestic fug, niggled by his frozen shoulder, his off-the-boil marriage, his disappearing step-daughter, but never quite enough to anything about any of them. At length, his hand his forced by a hostage-taking involving a former comrade from his own younger and more puritanical days. Lessing is, finally, a protagonist—albeit an unwilling, and rather cack-handed one.

So, if the women are anti-heroines, the men are hand-wringers. By way of explanation, Crace offers me one of his spiels. It's the writer's prerogative, he says: 'It's probably because I've got no interest in the men . . . I'm sitting in a room with characters I've created. Now, to some extent, as a person who has never committed adultery, this is an adulterous relationship. I'm creating women that I love.' But he does admit that there is more to it than that: 'Part of the issue in my life—and in English life, actually—is the conflict between feeble weakness—which is polite, and has all the protocols, and doesn't cause a stir, and doesn't harm anyone—and flashy violence and suchlike. I like weak characters.'

These are not revisionary fairy tales that attest to the temerity of the human spirit, then. And neither are they consolatory fictions; Crace is a naturalist, after all. In novels like *The Gift of Stones* and *Harvest* his version of pastoral is sublime and awe-inspiring, yes, but it is also brooding and sadistic or, worse, it simply *is*—impenetrable, indecipherable, and entirely beyond our reproach. The near-future urbanites of *Six* and *All That Follows*, for example, take to flaxseed, yoga and unsuccessful attempts to give up smoking as insurance against the inevitable. *Being Dead* unfurls from a random act of violence which gives the lie to all of this. The novel begins with a lengthy description of the death and decomposition of Joseph and Celice, murdered *in flagrante delicto*. It's delivered unflinchingly, and with biological precision. In these lives told backwards, structured according to an invented funeral ritual Crace calls 'quivering', there is redemption; but it's resolutely of this world and not the next.

'There was a reviewer who said I take a boyish delight in disgust and I couldn't work that out', he remembers, 'what she didn't get was that I'm not disgusted by that.' He explains: 'The optimism you can get by telling yourself lies is so easily achieved . . . It's so mawkish and it's a kind of comfort, but it's an optimism that is taken from a bright place, which is only inhabited by daffodils and tulips and rainbows. Whereas, my kind of optimism wants to find its place in the dark, in negative and difficult places, in dark corners of the universe.'

In *Being Dead*, Crace says he found his own 'narrative of comfort'. But he admits that he, too, is susceptible to the stories we tell ourselves. 'My father died in 1979 and he's dead, he's not anywhere. He was a walker and he was a birdwatcher and when I'm out walking I fantasise I meet him and we take a stroll together'. In fact it was this that was to be the subject of that final book that Crace could not finish, *Archipelago*. Again, the novel was the product of unlikely coincidence: two old photographs of Crace and his wife with their now-dead parents at the seaside that made an impossible pair. 'We both keep these pictures that seem to belong in the same landscape, we keep them in our diaries. I saw this and I thought I could invent somewhere, somewhere on the coast were you could find your mum and dad and it would be like *Gulliver's*

Travels. I'm excited even describing the book to you.' It would have made a contrary swansong; an autobiographical novel with a spiritual hook from this fibbing atheist. 'It was a case of real hubris, because I'm far too secretive a person to bring that novel off. I'm so secretive I couldn't even tell my wife', he admits. It might reappear at some point, as an '80-page Borgesian novel' (truth redacted, I presume), or as the natural history book his publishers want him to write next. But perhaps, for Crace, this is as fitting an ending as any: 'I've got the opposite of closure . . . I've got the adventure I was looking for.'

NOTES

[1] Jonathan Franzen, 'Jonathan Franzen: the path to Freedom', *Guardian*, May 25, 2012, http://www.guardian.co.uk/books/2012/may/25/jonathan-franzen-the-path-to-freedom.

[2] Dan Dennett, 'Why everyone is a novelist', *Times Literary Supplement*, September 16-22, 1988, 1029.

KATY SHAW

(Dis)locations: Post-Industrial Gothic in David Peace's Red Riding Quartet

The North is both our glory and our problem.
—Martin Wainwright

From Premier League football and police politics, to Noh drama and industrial disputes, the novels of David Peace offer "occult" accounts of twentieth-century British history.[1] Born in 1967, David Neil Peace was raised in Ossett, West Yorkshire. Schooled at Batley Grammar, Peace studied for A Levels at Wakefield Sixth Form College and went on to read English at Manchester Polytechnic, now Manchester Metropolitan University. After spending two years writing unpublished novels as an unemployed graduate, he left the UK in 1991 to teach English as a Foreign Language in Istanbul before moving to Tokyo in 1994. Peace has cited the importance of these travels in establishing a voice for his work. While living in Japan in 2003, he claimed that being 'far away now, it is perhaps easier for me to recreate and sustain the places and times about which I write—unimpeded and oblivious to the distractions and changes of the present'.[2] Peace lived in Tokyo until 2009 when he returned to Yorkshire with his Japanese wife and family. Published consecutively over a period of four years from 1999 to 2002, the novels of his *Red Riding Quartet*—entitled *1974, 1977, 1980* and *1983*—confront the secret past of Yorkshire and the UK during the 1970s and 1980s.[3] Exploring the darker side of humanity and society, the *Quartet* spans the North of England to chronicle an alternative account of the period of the hunt for the Yorkshire Ripper and the political ascendency of Prime Minister Margaret Thatcher.

Raking over uncomfortable histories, the canon of David Peace deliberately examines controversial people and contentious periods. Operating at the interface of fact and fiction, his texts break the surface of received histories, offering dense, noir-driven analyses of the contemporary world. Addressing the many and contradictory demands of history, of reality, truth and causality, as well as the confusions and debates that mask the power operating beneath overarching historical narratives, Peace's novels bleed fact into fiction as part of a wider move towards an evolving understanding of the past.

This essay will explore how and why Peace's *Red Riding Quartet* represents the North of England as both a place apart from the rest of the UK and the logical representation of its Gothic underside during the 1970s and 80s. Together, the four novels represent an effective no-man's land, a Yorkshire in transition and in dispute. Re-inscribing fresh meanings on an area historically defined by associations with the Brontës, the industrial revolution and heavy industry, the *Quartet* establishes a new post-industrial 'mythology of the North'.

There is something distinctly nightmarish, but hauntingly recognisable, about the North of England as represented through the eyes of David Peace. His fictional terrains expose readers to a strong sense of a place that defines itself through an innate difference from the rest of the country. This oppositional spatialisation posits the North of England as a counterbalance to the more 'civilised' South. In the *Red Riding Quartet*, the North is presented in an obstinate state of marginality, bound closely to issues of power and identity. Peace's North is 'as much a state of mind as a place', a space 'in England but never quite of it'.[4] Re-creating the bleak backdrop of a post-industrial UK, the four novels unite to present the North of England as a place of perpetually underlying anarchy, anxiety and sadism during the 1970s and 80s.

Since each novel offers a phase rather than a final ending, the UK is never whole or finalised in Peace's *Quartet*. Instead, it is broken into named counties that draw on oppositional relations to define one another. Peace does not offer a topographic map of the UK's regions but a fractured peremptory of them as conflicted and conflicting spaces. All counties have their own individual histories, associations and images but each also has an unspoken history, unseen images and illicit associations. Across the *Red Riding Quartet* regionalism is foregrounded in opposition to nationalism and counties confront one another as a means of reconfiguring psychic, social and cultural geographies.

The regional landscapes of the *Red Riding Quartet* are especially chilling because they are drawn at least in part from memories of the author's own childhood. Peace was born and raised in Ossett, West Yorkshire, and his novels can be viewed as a literary home-coming to this place. Peace has identified a 'homesickness in the *Red Riding Quartet*', a literary acknowledgement that 'the single biggest influence upon me was growing up when and where I did' even though it was 'not particularly fashionable to write about the North ... then or now'.[5] In many ways his *Quartet* evidences the claim that 'you can take the man out of Yorkshire but not ... Yorkshire out of the man!'[6] Peace recalls the Yorkshire of his youth as:

> a dark and dangerous and threatening place. It's in the very architecture and landscape of the place. This is at the ass end of industrialization. There was *massive* recession. It was a very bleak, ailing place. And then you had the contrast, as you went further North, and got out of the city, and then it got *very* very bleak. That's the scene of the Moors Murders. Everything seemed to be charged with some element of threat or danger ... it was more *enclosed,* and people were stressed.[7]

Throughout his work, Peace breaks down the doors of historically limited spaces and contentious times, employing landscape to make connections between socio-economic and geo-political conditions. Peace remains adamant that 'crime happens in specific times and places for specific reasons ... These things don't happen by chance. It wasn't the Cornwall Ripper, it was the Yorkshire Ripper; it happened here for a variety of very specific reasons that we don't want to look at any more'.[8] Turning back to the landscape of his youth, Peace uses the Northern English county of Yorkshire as a cultural and geographic site as well as a microcosm for the dark underside of the UK during the late twentieth century.

As the largest county in the UK, Yorkshire stretches over six thousand square miles of moorland, town and cities. Commonly known for its strong sense of regionalism and faith to 'county before country', it is divided into three Ridings (meaning 'divisions of a county'), North, East and West. Representing 1970s and 1980s Yorkshire as an area steeped in evil and corruption, Peace offers a mythologising portrait of place. Created by more than simply topographical factors, the county of Yorkshire exists in a climate of fear that is described as specifically Northern. Fear and paranoia in the region gradually extend to the country at large as the crisis becomes national. As Ripper writer Michael Bilton argues, 'You have to live in the North of England to comprehend how such a terrible series of crimes terrified a major part of the British Isles' since 'vast swathes of the North of England were affected by the complete absence of peaceful communities during the Ripper case'.[9]

Peace's vision of his home county circles around shared traumas and times, listing a monotonous history of destruction and death. Challenging popular representations of Yorkshire as 'God's own country', the *Quartet* instead presents a secluded community characterised by parochialism and defiance. Here, it is 1970 going on the Dark Ages, Peace's 'poisoned pastoral' reflecting the fallout created by social and political unrest.[10] A Right-wing agenda, industrial collapse, religious and racial conflicts, misogyny and economic recession manifest themselves in a Yorkshire struggling to cope with the unwanted effects of change. From this chaos, the Yorkshire Ripper emerges as a Gothic monster and an image of disorder. Peter Sutcliffe, dubbed by the UK media the 'Yorkshire Ripper', killed thirteen women in Yorkshire from 1975 to 1980, casting a shadow over the county for nearly a decade before his arrest in 1981. Re-visiting these crimes and their times as a shadowy expression of the social, political and economic ills of the 1970s and 80s, Peace uses Yorkshire and the Ripper as a lens through which to re-examine the period.

During a twentieth century of industrial decline, Yorkshire turned 'from the avatar of modernisation into a byword for backwardness'.[11] A combination of deindustrialisation and suburbanisation during the 1970s and 80s produced a power vacuum in Yorkshire leading to urban decay and abandoned spaces inhabited by marginalised people. Peace focuses on the ways in which this moral and spiritual decline extends outwards through the built environment.

The gradual erasure of heavy industry is evidenced in the disappearance of structures from the skyline. Although the economy began a post-industrial shift during the 1970s and 80s, Peace's Yorkshire refuses to move forwards and continues to lag behind the rest of the UK. Through his historical inflections, Peace raises the ghosts of Britain's former industrial glory against the ubiquity of modern developments to offer alienated voices of despair and loss. The bleakness of a county reliant on dying industries creates a tangible sense of the 1970s and 80s as a period of 'winters and hate. Darkness and fear'.[12]

The social engineering of 'urban regeneration' programmes that seek to replace these old landscapes is arguably the real crime at the heart of the *Quartet*, as underhand coppers and developers adopt the coy euphemisms of 'business opportunities' and 'agreements' to justify their underground operations. Like many organisations in the *Red Riding Quartet*, Yorkshire's construction industry is shown to be highly localised and extremely corrupt. Its logical development is represented in conspiratorial plans to finance and erect a new Ridings Shopping Centre using the dual resources of building know-how and police vice funds. Evidencing a desire for status, power and independence inherent in Peace's Yorkshire, this temple to capitalism and consumption is founded upon corruption. By means of social critique, glimpses are provided of the effects the new centre will have on the established space of the local community, granting the reader an additional dimension of decline in the demise of smaller independent and family-run local businesses.

Focussing on what lies beneath, Peace draws attention to the historical, cultural and social processes through which the environment is shaped. Visualising a landscape in transition, his *Quartet* sets architectural space against natural space, encouraging readers to observe 'overlooked' elements of Yorkshire life. Characters move across the Moors to highlight revealed and concealed worlds. Through these subterranean sites Peace explores meditative spaces that illuminate gaps between physical experience and visual perception. In a dark, alternative world of still life, underground spaces position Yorkshire as a place of rape and rhubarb, a site of production and consumption, pleasure and pain.

In the *Red Riding Quartet*, Yorkshire is presented as a potent hybrid of surface and subterranea, urban and rural, staunchly barren in both climate and physical composition. Re-inscribing the meaning of a well-known landscape, Peace's Moors form the grounds upon which narrative events unfold. Historically, the Yorkshire Moors have enjoyed a mythology of space, authenticity and strength. The *Red Riding Quartet* underscores their savage power, but also offers the Moors as a site of sub-human actions.

The symbolic backdrop of the Yorkshire Moors is confronted through a natural world that is resoundingly brown, burnt out and barren. Peace seems to struggle for language adequate to represent this space. Any associations with the Brontës and windswept heather are quickly brushed aside by his novels. Peace's depiction of the Moors evidences a kind of anti-Romanticism, a refusal to celebrate landscape. The beauty of nature cannot thrive in this environment, cannot co-exist with a Thatcherite society. Confronting historical constructions of Yorkshire and its Moors and undermining established mythic associations, Peace's aesthetic sensibility does not allow for meaningful experiences with nature. Instead, his vision of Yorkshire is of a deeply foreboding, shadowy world that betrays the wider corruptions of the county and country.

A rain-swept vision of Yorkshire reaches its zenith in Leeds. Peace's fictional Leeds is a dark, violent and masculine place, described in taut lyrical prose as the back-drop to much of his work. In Leeds readers witness the iconography of landscape through architecture, an exterior surface of history set against an interior of meaning and experience. Peace recalls that as a child 'Leeds itself seemed to me to be very dark and very depressing (and where they filmed the exteriors for *A Clockwork Orange*). I never felt at ease there and the buildings seemed almost "haunted"—the Dark Arches, the Griffin Hotel, the Millgarth Police Station, the various shopping centres, and Elland Road'.[13] Signs of Gothic decay and serious post-industrial economic damage are visually inflicted on the landscape of his fictional Leeds. Buildings and bodies litter this landscape, charting a series of interlocking crises: the disintegration of the city and society and the consequences of the defeat of socialism, modernism and ideas of progress.

Ceaselessly questioning the past and present via familiar vistas, Peace interrogates the city's history of medieval torture and punishment, empire and power, industry and revolution. Subject to constant struggles for power, the chiming bells of jubilation transport the reader back to a present of monarchic celebration. However, these celebrations do not extend to the characters of *Red Riding*; instead Peace focuses on primal flames of discontent. Offering tortured visions of a place and the ghosts that inhabit it, his built and imagined environments interact with one another via established historical associations of inner city Leeds. The *Quartet* draws upon this architectural uncanny to form a haunto-topography. Mapping a landscape of spectral sites, frequent injections into the narratives of street names and addresses encourage the reader to form a geographical awareness of this space. Working from models of reality, fantasy and memory, Peace knits fact and fiction into an expression of time and place to produce landscapes that are more than a reproduction of the obvious or familiar. In a city marred by destruction, atrophy and decay, a stultifying atmosphere combines with emotionally charged spaces to speak to the depths of characters' minds. As they gradually become overwhelmed by the pressures of events, Peace's Leeds becomes part of their suffering.

Peace rakes over the said but also the necessarily 'unsaid' horror of the post-industrial Gothic to offer a culturally determined psychology of Northern England as a place of confrontation. Peace's North is a museum of time and place, a space invested with human meaning and codified history. As a grim site of regional devotion, it offers a distinct counter-narrative on an alternative, yet insistent, past. Throughout the *Quartet*, landscape is employed as an articulating vestige of experience, representing 'many interwoven layers of power . . . race, gender, class and local identity politics'.[14] Brannigan argues that the 'representation of landscape in literary texts . . . is related to and embedded in social and political structures'.[15] While many spaces become charged with meanings over time, the *Red Riding Quartet* takes pains to show how social, economic and cultural deterioration can shape the image of a region, both reflecting and articulating social periphery and geographic marginality.

In an environment of threat and neglect scarred by fragmentation both physical and metaphoric, Peace grants symbolic dimensions to space. However, his vision is not one of provincialism. In his *Quartet*, Yorkshire and the North of England are presented as diffuse and decentralised but specific in terms of environment and socio-cultural anxieties about relationalism. Vistas emerge from the anxieties of the characters and the people of the regions as sites of atrocity and places of memory. Re-mapping the psycho-geography of the UK during the 1970s and 80s, Peace reconfigures previous assumptions as well as inscribing new meanings to well-known places and spaces. Re-visioning familiar landscapes as a means of accessing a psychological inscape of suffering, psychosis and trauma, Peace uses space as an extension or manifestation of his characters' doubts and fears. Illuminating memories carved into the built and natural environment, his novels offer Yorkshire of the 1970s and 1980s as a dynamic site of memory and meaning.

Collectively, the *Red Riding Quartet* not only offers a political representation of landscape, but landscape as a political form of representation. Localising his representations of 1970s and 80s Britain in the social, economic and political contexts of de-industrialisation and the psychological and literary contexts of a profound Gothic inheritance, Peace documents a geography of the imagination, but also of the recognisable physical world. Through his fictional landscapes, Peace enters into a wider debate concerning trauma, the uncertainty of the present and a legacy of displacement and fracture. His desolate tableau layers terrors and dream images, accentuating troubled and traumatic narratives. Excavating and altering familiar landscapes, his novels question the origins of these places and in doing so establish new formal and thematic relationships. Provoking unease and revelation, Yorkshire and the North of England are represented in unexpected new lights to create disturbing juxtapositions. Setting Leeds against the Moors and Yorkshire against a wider (dis)United Kingdom, the *Quartet* interrogates physical and psychological relationships to suggest that while literary landscapes can be knowable places, they remain impossible to definitively 'locate'.

NOTES

[1] Opening quotation from Martin Wainwright, *True North* (London: Guardian, 2009), 10.

[2] David Peace, 'Talking Books: David Peace May 2003', *BBC Online*, http://www.bbc.co.uk/bradford/culture/words/david_peace_intv.shtml, accessed 19 May 2004.

[3] All references to the novels of David Peace contained in this book refer to the following paperback editions: *1974* (London: Serpent's Tail, 1999); *1977* (London: Serpent's Tail, 2000); *1980* (London: Serpent's Tail, 2001); *1983* (London: Serpent's Tail, 2002); *GB84*, (London: Faber, 2004); *The Damned United* (London: Faber, 2007); *Tokyo Year Zero* (London: Faber, 2008); *Occupied City* (London: Faber, 2010).

[4] J. Hill and J. Williams, 'Sport and Identity in the North of England', *Regional Identities*, ed. E. Royale (Manchester: Manchester University Press, 1998), 201; A. Mitchell, 'Manifesto of The North', *The English Question*, ed. T. Wright (London: Fabian Society, 2000), 46.

[5] David Peace, 'The Big Issue Event: Q&A with Paul Johnston', *Edinburgh Book Festival*, 22 August 2009; David Peace, 'In Conversation with Kester Aspen', *Waterstones* Leeds Q&A to launch *Occupied City*, 13 August 2009.

[6] Roy Wright, 'Huddersfield Town fan David Peace is behind TV's darkest tale', *Huddersfield Daily Examiner*, 5 March 2009.

[7] David Peace, 'h2g2 BBC Author: David Peace', *BBC Online*, http://www.bbc.co.uk/dna/h2g2/A3126188, accessed 10 August 2009.

[8] David Peace in Nicola Upson, 'Hunting The Yorkshire Ripper', *New Statesman*, 20 Aug 2001, http://www.newstatesman.com/200108200036, accessed 10 April 2008.

[9] Michael Bilton, *Wicked Beyond Belief: the Hunt for the Yorkshire Ripper* (London: Harper Collins, 2006), xxxi; 582.

[10] David Thomson in LeftBank Pictures, *The Damned United Production Notes* (London: LeftBank Pictures, 2009), 9.

[11] Raphael Samuel, *Theatres of Memory: Vol II Island Stories* (London: Verso, 1998), 166.

[12] David Peace, 'Profile', *The Telegraph*, http://www.telegraph.co.uk/culture/tvandradio/4980191/David-Peace-author-of-Red-Riding-and-The-Damned-United-

profile.html, accessed 10 August 2009.

[13] David Peace, 'Book Munch Classic Interview: David Peace', *Bookmunch*, http://www.bookmunch.co.uk/view.php?id=1341, accessed 10 August 2009.

[14] Greg Ashworth and Brian Graham (eds.), *Sense of Place: Sense of Time*, (Aldershot: Ashgate, 2005), 70.

[15] John Brannigan, *Orwell To The Present: Literature In England 1945-2000*, (Basingstoke: Palgrave Macmillan, 2003), 174.

STEWART HOME

HUMANITY WILL NOT BE HAPPY UNTIL THE LAST MAN BOOKER PRIZE WINNER IS HUNG BY THE GUTS OF THE FINAL RECIPIENT OF THE NOBEL PRIZE FOR LITERATURE!

Literature today functions as a giant Ponzi scheme. It is worthless but those who've invested time in it have to convince others to involve themselves in this scam in order to recoup something from it. Most successful writers subscribe to the backward worldview of the bourgeoisie because they are more interested in being celebrities than in writing worthwhile books. These hacks promote and backslap each other and do everything possible to prevent vibrant writing from reaching the reading public. Those who have been awarded so-called "honours" such as the Man Booker or Nobel prizes should be especially despised (even when they refuse them—since as all reasonable people know, it is completely unacceptable to produce work that merits such prizes). Time will judge today's literary celebrities very harshly—or to put it another way, they will very quickly be completely forgotten.

The conventional novel is the most favoured and privileged cultural vehicle of bourgeois ideology—although obviously it would be pretty useless were it not backed up by the army and the police force (i.e., might). The emphasis on character in the novel reflects the bourgeois conception of the individual as the sole proprietor of his or her skills and as owing nothing to society. These skills (and those of others) are presented to the reader as a commodity to be bought and sold on the open market in a society where a solipsistic and unending thirst for consumption is considered the crucial core of human nature. These ideas found their clearest articulation in the non-fiction of liberal political writers such as Hobbes, Harrington and Locke; but they have also formed the bedrock of bourgeois literary fiction for the past two hundred years.

Bourgeois hacks like Julian Barnes and Ian McEwan represent a world we must leave behind. Those embracing progressive political positions are against nation states and have no time for the idea of England, whereas these hacks want to deny the power of the international working class and thus fixate on national issues and so-called "national differences". Their bad writing follows on from their reactionary political views and vice versa—each flows from the other. Those that want to defend a discredited capitalist system can't write well, they have to obfuscate. To take two further examples, the prose of Salman Rushdie and Martin Amis is just as awful as that of Barnes and McEwan. Both are products of exclusive schools and Oxbridge, and neither have anything to say that is worth hearing. They don't know the first thing about how ordinary people live and they don't know how to write. But they are typical of the talentless posh boys promoted by the English literary establishment.

Proletarians prefer to use direct language so that their meaning is clear. They say what they want to say as simply as possible. That said, a complex idea requires more complex expression. In other words it is easier to say "fuck off" than it is to articulate a critique of commodity production and capitalist alienation. Nonetheless, truly contemporary writers try to keep things straightforward and at the minimum necessary level of complexity for what they wish to articulate. Literary writers do the opposite, their defences of bourgeois society are really very simple and not at all convincing, which is why they try to dress them up in unnecessarily mannered and complex language. In this and all other senses literature is decadent. And it is also why in the long run literature stands no chance against those who have learnt the collective strength "secrets" of the proletarian superwomen.

It is not a matter of doing away with the culture of the past in its entirety, but rather of bringing selected parts of it back into play. In many ways so much has now been written that all we need to do is plunder and rewrite what's already online and this is in fact the basis of new movements in the anti-arts such as conceptual literature and Flarf poetry. It is no longer a question of writing but of editing—and editing with a complete disregard for the logic and narrative structure of the texts we plunder. As the Lettrists declared back in the 1950s, the cultural heritage of mankind should be cut-up and used for partisan political purposes.

Anti-literature or art novels are often erroneously judged on the same criteria as literary works; this is ridiculous because truly contemporary writers long ago abandoned the Cartesian dualism, fetish for logical plot and ridiculous obsession with character that mark the bourgeois novel out as backward. In anti-literature delirium is often favoured to an over-analytical (i.e., boring) emphasis on plot development. One way of overcoming the cold logic of bourgeois novels is to repeat the same simple plot tricks again and again, in book after book—until finally the notion of salvation through plot or the resolution of a puzzle (in terms of the detective genre) becomes meaningless. Plots come to be what Alain Robbe-Grillet calls "generators". That is to say they are jumping off points for both author and reader into a shared world of wonder, terror and "spectacle".

What these "generators" do is open doors for the reader into new non-linear and non-logical structures for fiction. Common reference points give the audience a sense of familiarity and free the writer from the need to logically underscore each plot point. A series of loosely connected dramatic building blocks can be used to construct new ways of telling stories. Once we discover there are millions of new ways in which we can write, it should also be apparent by analogy that there are many new ways in which we could organise the world. It should go without saying that we can sample and adapt other authors—as I have in this and the preceding paragraph (having drawn here on Pete Tombs and Cathal Tohill's discussion of European sex and horror cinema in their book *Immoral Tales*).

Most people don't require any specialised knowledge to enjoy anti-writing— as long as they haven't been brainwashed into thinking about "literature" in the restricted sense of bourgeois subjectivity. Those who think that books are about linear plot and plodding characterisation will have a real problem with anti-literature. They can only be likened to people who think paintings have to be representational. These dim-wits are living in the past and they're completely incapable of understanding contemporary culture. Aside from over-"educated" plonkers of this stripe, most contemporary readers have few if any problems understanding anti-literature. The more educational qualifications someone has, the lower their ability to understand the world and the culture being produced in it today. It is well known that university education drives down intellectual standards, and that professors tend to be the biggest dullards of the lot.

The poverty of university life is in part due to academics being so dependent upon other specialists within their area for career advancement. As a consequence most are afraid to shake things up and organise material into new paradigms or view it from new perspectives—no matter how erroneous the academic consensus on any particular subject may be. Similarly, the didactic and hierarchical nature of university teaching clearly discourages critical thinking among students. Acting as if they are somehow stuck in the nineteenth century, most university professors attempt to position themselves as experts handing down truths from on high. Year in and year out such attitudes serve to ensure there is an intellectually inert and docile crop of graduates and postgraduates.

This contrasts sharply with the learning environment provided by online sites such as Wikipedia, which despite their many faults are not reliant on the kind of conformism essential to academic success. The ongoing expansion of university education has contributed a great deal to the impoverished state of contemporary writing, since publishing and criticism are at present dominated by university graduates. Worse yet are English department-based so-called creative writing courses, which place a premium value on all the outmoded literary conceits that students need to jettison before they can produce anything worthwhile.

Returning to anti-writing, it is a discontinuous tradition that predates literature and that encompasses black humour, theory and experimentation with both prose and poetic forms. One could cite anything from Laurence Sterne's *Tristram Shandy*, to the works of Kathy Acker by way of Karl Marx as examples of this form. The important thing is not to be restricted by the genre known as literary fiction.

Most of the living writers promoted as being worthwhile by the bourgeois press and universities are in fact utterly tedious, and this is precisely because they project themselves as being serious. To do anything worthwhile writers have to get over the adolescent mania for being po-faced, grow up and grow into humour and laughs. The adolescent thinks that to be an adult you have to always act like a grown-up—whereas the precise opposite is the case. To be properly grown up and to do anything really serious you have to do it with humour and levity. There are just way too many middle-aged literary writers out there whose misplaced sense of "gravity" and importance reveals them to still have the minds of adolescents. Only anti-literature attains the levity that is a necessary corollary to real gravity.

The conventional bourgeois novel is socially conservative and is all about reproducing the ideas and subjectivities of the dominant class—that is why it is so concerned with what is euphemistically called "character". And while bourgeois novels don't reflect the world we live in, they exhibit an obsession with realism, naturalism and nineteenth-century ideas about narrative because these are the distortions and blinkers through which the ruling class wishes us to misperceive the world. Just breaking with such nonsense is political. Unfortunately traditional and outmoded literary ideas dominate not only publishing but also much criticism and teaching. As a consequence those who reject its silly abstractions are constantly asked to explain why.

Recently in an in an interview with a Spanish journalist I was asked: 'Aren't you interested in making literature in a traditional way? What "tricks" or "vices" don't you like in the literary tradition?' I answered: 'This question reveals a lot about how backward literature has become. I think it unlikely you'd ask an artist why they didn't want to paint like Goya or Velázquez. Certainly when I talk about the art work I do in galleries I'm never asked questions like this. People understand that visual art has moved on over the past few centuries. Why would I want to write like nineteenth-century novelists such as Charles Dickens or Jane Austen? Aside from the fact that I find such writing both boring and reactionary, those who still produce superannuated prose of this type are expected to behave as if they are dull and square (which, since they mostly are, obviously isn't a problem for the sad sacks still writing nineteenth-century literature today). The public image of the serious writer requires that they don't do the sort of things I like to do—such as standing on my head before reciting passages from my books when I appear in public. By way of contrast I like Goya and Velázquez but there is no point in painting like them now—they did their own period very well and we have to (un)make art for our own.'

In the middle of the last century William Burroughs and Brion Gysin introduced the cut-up to writing in an attempt to update it, comparing what they were doing to collage and saying that literature was fifty years behind art. Today, those who insist that painting should be realistic and representational are treated as a laughing stock. Sadly the same is not true of those who demand realism (which is an ideology and not at all the same thing as reality) and naturalism in fiction, with the result that writing has now fallen more than a hundred years behind art.

Although Burroughs attacked the commodity in the form of addictive drugs in his prose, where he and Gysin fail us is in not extending this critique of commodification explicitly to the realm of culture and proceeding to view the role of the writer and artist dialectically. Anyone who understands that disalienation is integral to the communist project also knows that to become truly human we have to realise every aspect of what we are—what is sometimes called our 'species being'. Aside from being social that also means integrating our physical, emotional and intellectual activity. So rather than one person being a brain worker (white collar) and another performing physical labour (blue collar), in a classless society (which will also be one without money and nation states), we'll all do a bit of everything and have a lot of variety in our lives. To look at the roles of the artist and prose fiction writer in a positive light, it is a deformed prefiguration of how we'll all be in post-capitalist society. But artists and prose fiction writers are also specialised non-specialists in a commodified gallery and publishing system, so you can also look at that role negatively and stress its alienation and disconnection from what it is to be truly human.

There is no future for the type of bourgeois literary fiction that dominates publishing today. Writers who treat their readers like idiots—and, for example, when they make a joke feel compelled to heavy-handedly signal this—must be thrown on the scrapheap of history. Anti-literature by way of contrast credits its readers with intelligence and imagination, and provides them with more freedom than they'd find in the dead literature of the ruling class. The reader can fill in gaps and the resultant juxtapositions can be funny, beautiful or startling. Readers can take these any which way they want—but they also have to accept responsibility for their readings.

While anti-writers have no interest in the ideology of realism, the fragmented style they use is in fact closer to what we experience in daily life than the tediously even tone of conventional literature. Our minds flip from one thought to another, we flick through channels on TV and move from stories about the massacres in Homs to documentaries on the sex life of rare sea species, and from that to gymnastic and cycling competitions, and on to shopping channels and chat shows. Such flipping from one thing to another can be done like a sleepwalker, or it can be done critically and consciously.

The profits to be made from films, books and music, have declined greatly with the rise of the internet. This is a good thing because it has resulted in such pursuits being of less interest to those who merely wish to make money and/or become celebrities. Those of us wanting to develop proletarian culture into something even more revolutionary will keep doing what we've always been doing and we'll become even more effective at it. The most immediate impediment to the ongoing development of vibrant and exciting contemporary writing practices remains the institutional dominance of the so-called "educated" classes, since these brainwashed zombies are living in the past and continue to cultivate a completely reactionary bourgeois subjectivity through both literature and other means.

CAROLE JONES

Post-Meta-Modern-Realism: The Novel in Scotland

Scottish novel writing presents us with a heterogeneous field of enquiry which has regularly outwitted attempts to contain it within a literary scheme. The 1994 Booker Prize for Fiction demonstrated this in arresting fashion when it produced a provocative Scottish coup; not only was the winner James Kelman's *How Late It Was, How Late*, but it was joined on the shortlist by George Mackay Brown's *Beside the Ocean of Time*. The infamous uproar accompanying Kelman's win blasted his use of a Glasgow voice and an alarming number of swear words. Brown's novel could not have provided more of a contrast to Kelman's urban sprawl; *Beside the Ocean of Time* is set on the fictional Orkney island of Norday and evokes the mythic Nordic past as well as the devastating World War Two history of those islands. Tightly structured, lyrical, elegiac and poetic in its engagement with the landscape and island life, the novel and its traditionally omniscient storyteller narrator are in many ways the opposite of Kelman's contemporary Glasgow seen through the complexly presented consciousness of his blinded protagonist Sammy Samuels.

It is possible to characterise these writers as exemplary of two diverse polarities, some would say contradictions, of Scottish writing, a tradition famous for both realism and romance, frequently in the same work. Kelman is more often read as a realist, representing city-bound working-class lives and voices of the present time in an uncompromising vernacular which forces the reader to see the world from the point of view of his all-male cast of protagonists. Brown is celebrated for his association with Orkney, is seen, in fact, as the islands' literary representative and consistently portrays his rural home in his poetry and fiction. *Beside the Ocean of Time* is the story of Thorfinn Ragnarson, a young dreamer through whom the reader encounters stories evoking Orcadian myth and history, from the distant Nordic past to the battle of Bannockburn to seal wives and their strange ways. The latter part of the novel relates the devastation of Norday in the Second World War when it is turned into an airbase for the British Air Force. Thorfinn, now a writer, eventually returns to the deserted island after his experience as a prisoner of war and contemplates the creation of the 'unattainable poem' of his birthplace. History and biography entwine with myth, folklore and an abiding interest in ritual in Brown's writing constructing a sensibility more often placed within the romance region of the Scottish tradition.

However, on closer, more patient examination the polarities begin to break down and contradictory characteristics emerge. Brown, with his enduring belief in myth, can be conceived of as a modernist writer on a quest for 'a universally applicable value system'.[1] Yet Schoene believes that Brown is 'a modernist writer with postmodernist tendencies' where 'his resolute conflation of fact and fiction, his disregard for generic boundaries and his firm belief in the text as a means of reconciling disparate aspects of an essentially discontinuous reality'[2] are all postmodern features of his work. His artistry is never disputed. In contrast, Kelman, seen as a quintessential working-class writer, is by that definition artless in directly disgorging his experience onto paper in an unmediated manner. Of course, this hackneyed perception is thankfully fading now and Kelman's radical stylistic innovation is more widely valued. The interiority of his work, with its stream-of-consciousness sensibility, is qualified by disorientating slippages of pronouns and linguistic registers, placing his narrative voice on the boundary between the internal and external worlds of his protagonists. Kelman's taking up of this modernist strategy draws attention to the instability of texts and the selves they represent and defies grounding categorisation. Take the opening of *How Late It Was, How Late*:

> Ye wake in a corner and stay there hoping yer body will disappear, the thoughts smothering ye; these thoughts; but ye want to remember and face up to things, just something keeps ye from doing it, why can ye no do it; the words filling yer head: then the other words; there's something wrong; there's something far far wrong; ye're no a good

man, ye're just no a good man. Edging back into awareness, of where
ye are: here, slumped in this corner, with these thoughts filling ye.
And oh christ his back was sore; stiff, and the head pounding. He
shivered and hunched up his shoulders, shut his eyes, rubbed into
the corners with his fingertips; seeing all kinds of spots and lights.
Where in the name of fuck . . . [3]

This seems to me to fulfil Virginia Woolf's exhortation to the fiction writer
to 'look within' and 'examine for a moment an ordinary mind on an ordinary
day'.[4] The extract moves from an alienated interiority to third person objective description to direct expression, perhaps, in the final statement. In his
work Kelman's signature use of free indirect discourse creates a vacillating
boundary of selfhood, not a socially constructed automaton but not wholly
a self-defining agent either; this technique bears comparison with Woolf's
radical literary form in her texts of "high modernism". The contradiction
projected by the combination of this pejoratively labelled bourgeois style—
notwithstanding its presentation of working-class language and culture—and
Kelman's politically committed working-class image produces consternation
and denial in some quarters.

Contradiction is no stranger to the Scottish tradition which, as hinted
above, is stereotypically contrived to hone itself out of oppositional creative
modes and has made serious play with the destabilising of generic boundaries. This was previously seen as the mark of an inferior tradition, but in
what is now known as the devolutionary period this changed. Devolution,
or the transfer of powers from the Parliament at Westminster to a Scottish
legislative assembly, was put to the vote in Scotland in a referendum in 1979,
which failed, and in 1997, which succeeded, paving the way for the re-in-
stating of the Scottish Parliament in 1999 for the first time since the Act of
Union in 1707. In the interim, devolutionary stage between the referenda,
Scottish writing embraced and even exaggerated the hybridity of the tradition
'in what, retrospectively, appears as a deliberate act of artistic devolution—if
not, indeed, as a declaration of cultural independence'.[5] Writers revelled in an
experimental freedom which broke down the boundaries of the text generi-

cally, formally and typographically, taking inspiration from Alasdair Gray's epoch-setting novel *Lanark: A Life in Four Books* (1981). Here, with a heady, deliberate mixing of realism and fantasy, the traditionally conceived novelistic form of progressing time and plot gave way to a radical refashioning: Book Four followed Book Two which came after Book One which was placed after the opening Book Three; the Prologue occurs at the end of Book Three and the Epilogue in the midst of Book Four, where the author appears and argues with the protagonist as to the resolution of the narrative, accompanied by an 'Index of Plagiarisms'. Such hectic experimentalism has since been relished as exemplarily postmodern, a new exulting in the instabilities and fragmentations of Scottish identity and culture which in themselves could now be thought of as positively and fashionably postmodern.

In *Lanark*, however, Gray's message was also a political one; at the heart of the novel is a critique of the destructive effects of capitalism. As Linda Hutcheon argued in a significant and apt critical intervention, contradiction is central to postmodernism, but it is also 'unavoidably political'.[6] In the Scottish context the outburst of literary experimentation in devolutionary fiction was never less than politically motivated, expressive of an ethical impulse to represent the marginalised and the outsider and give space to their suppressed voices. As Kelman said, expressing the sentiments of many other writers, 'I wanted to write and remain a member of my community'.[7] Cairns Craig proclaims that 'the explosion of writing in Scots after 1984 was effectively a devolution of the word, asserting at the level of culture an independence as yet unachieved at the level of politics'.[8] The embrace of the insights of a postmodern sensibility arguably transformed the reading of Scottish novels, as well as the writing of them, into acts of radicalism.

The new century, however, has instituted a sobering of attitudes casting doubt on the integrity and even possibility of a political postmodernism. A backlash against the discourse has become more vocal in the last decade and books such as Jose Lopez and Gary Potter's *After Postmodernism* (2001) and Klaus Stierstorfer's *Beyond Postmodernism* (2003), for example, conceive of the cultural phenomenon insistently in the past tense. There is a perception, or a desire even, that we are *beyond postmodernism*. Such a scenario raises crucial questions for a Scottish cultural scene which, as we have seen, has much invested in the analytical power and sensibilities of the discourse. With the authority of a blandly instituted postmodernism now undermined, the question arises whether emergent cultural forces in writing and publishing posit a return to more uncomplicated representational tenets such as those of a conservative realism? Such fears were voiced by Kelman himself in 2009 in a rare appearance at the Edinburgh International Book Festival when he attacked the dominance and media hype of genre fiction; he polemicized that '[i]f the Nobel Prize came from Scotland they would give it to a writer of fucking detective fiction,'[9] a reference to the popularity of crime writing in Scotland. Kelman's intervention caused a gleeful media outcry and split the literary establishment. However, his outburst prompts critical questions about the ethical implications of cultural strategies, especially one known for its radical relativism and experiments in anti-realism.

Certainly a major constituency of Scottish writers continues to advocate experimenting with formal and thematic possibilities. Kelman himself in *Keiron Smith, Boy* (2008) and authors such as Alan Warner in *The Stars in the Bright Sky* (2010) produce thoughtfully constructed and complex meditations on the radically defamiliarizing power of language, particularly here in relation to the world of young people. The challenge to the fixity of identities implicit in anti-realist textual strategies remains a fundamental concern of much contemporary writing. As Glaswegian Suhayl Saadi says about his own work, 'I aimed to promote syncretism, liminality and heteroglossia in order to dynamise ideas of social class, ethnicity, history, musicality, geography and consciousness.'[10] Ali Smith, a writer who is often not associated with a Scottish context, maintains a Scottish presence in her vividly original novels. For example, in *The Accidental* (2006) the mysterious figure Amber, the disruptive force who creates havoc in the middle-class family she unaccountably lands in, is Scottish, preserving the unsettling effect of the disquieting romance facet of the Scottish tradition. And her latest novel, *There But For The* (2011), opening with a Scottish character, continues to pose philosophical questions regarding the nature of storytelling and representation in a teasingly meta-fictional exploration of memory and communication, intersubjectivity and belief. Connecting these writers is a commitment to a politics of representation which involves challenging complacent ways of seeing and portraying the world. Though we may not refer to this as a unified postmodern body of work, all these authors deploy strategies associated with the iconoclastic impulses of postmodernism.

These concerns are foregrounded in A.L. Kennedy's writing which highlights the dilemma that has come to surround the ethics of postmodernism. Though her narratives are praised for her deft rendering of her metafictional preoccupations with the purpose of writing, this appraisal is often quickly qualified by reference to the ethical seriousness of her method and intent; her stylistic expertise is not 'an empty technical exercise or a display of postmodern knowingness, but rather works in the service of some more traditional, humanistic purpose'.[11] The imputation here of the lesser moral intent and effect of postmodern writing implies that an ethical discourse can only be adequately realised in more humanist modes which deal in a recognisable world of referents and values, and a shared reality. Kennedy's fiction, however, does not promote the return to a straightforward humanist discourse but employs the techniques of postmodernism to counter its own most radical effects. Her work does not present a singular, indisputable reality or truth, but invites us to arrive at an ethical interpretation of an ambivalently depicted situation; postmodern literary writing enables this precisely because of its privileged doubleness and irony. An emotive example is found in the story 'As God Made Us' from the collection *What Becomes* (2009). Here a teacher berates a group of amputees, survivors of recent and ongoing military campaigns, for attending a swimming pool, telling them their disabilities cause upset. She has told her school-children the men are 'as god made' them,[12] a distortion of the facts of their plight which suppresses the violent reality embodied in the men. However, depending on your political and spiritual beliefs (you may view current conflicts as modern "crusades", for instance) the teacher's is not a completely inarguable position; it is, though, ethically unsustainable as her treatment of the men as less human, as monstrous, explicitly determines.

Kennedy rejects the language and sensibility of postmodernism when she asserts that literature is a redemptive and humanising practice. Because of its potential as a point of communal unity, an occasion for communication, togetherness and contact between individuals, it provides an opportunity to overcome the postmodern relativism and disconnection which Kennedy perceives as structuring the world. Yet this is not because of its presentation of enduring truthful depictions of that world, but because art is an occasion of contestation—of meaning and interpretation. Kennedy promotes belief, or faith even, in this power of art, an attitude which places her contra both the rationalism of humanism and the aversion to grand narratives which characterises postmodernism. The magic, Kennedy would aver, is not in the message of a text but in its prompting of human communication and convergence, an awareness and experience of intersubjectivity. In her latest novel, *The Blue Book* (2011), she makes the theme of magic central by depicting a fake medium, a symbol of the writer with the power to create convincing illusions. This can be done for morally correct or questionable reasons—the addressing and possible alleviating of individual trauma or the medium's personal financial gain—highlighting the crucial ethical choices at the heart of the illusionist's craft. Though not grounded in a stable, singularly understood reality this art of faking creates the opportunity for the experience of coherent selfhood and community, a delusion of humanist truth and intersubjective understanding which, even if it is only momentary, provides a basis for the good life.

All the works referred to here are examples of a Scottish writing scene which challenges the humanist premises of realism but employs a postmodern sensibility, if not postmodern literary strategies, to highlight the ethical dilemmas left in the wake of the dismantling of certainties enacted in recent decades. Their yearning towards stability and truth is expressed through acceptance of the impossibility of that quest. In the near future we may be describing such work with new terms such as "metarealism"[13] or "metamodernism".[14] For the moment I will simply pay tribute to the restless experimental spirit which displaces these texts beyond easy limitation and labelling and confounds categories and categorisation in line with the best custom and practice of the Scottish tradition.

NOTES

[1] Berthold Schoene, *The Making of Orcadia: Narrative Identity in the Prose Work of George Mackay Brown* (Frankfurt am Main: Peter Lang, 1995), 270.

[2] Ibid.

[3] James Kelman, *How Late It Was, How Late* (London: Vintage, 1998), 1.

[4] Virginia Woolf, 'Modern Fiction', in *Selected Essays*, ed. David Bradshaw (Oxford: Oxford University Press, 2008), 9.

[5] Cairns Craig, 'Devolving the Scottish Novel', in *A Concise Companion to Contemporary British Fiction*, ed. James F. English (Oxford: Blackwell, 2006), 128.

[6] Linda Hutcheon, *The Politics of Postmodernism* (London: Routledge, 1999), 1.

[7] James Kelman, 'The Importance of Glasgow in My Work', in *Some Recent Attacks: Essays Cultural and Political* (Stirling: AK Press, 1992), 81.

[8] Cairns Craig, 'Devolving the Scottish Novel', 135.

[9] Phil Miller, 'Kelman blasts mediocrity of boy wizards and crime bestsellers', *Herald*, August 27, 2009.

[10] Suhayl Saadi, 'In Tom Paine's Kitchen: Days of Rage and Fire', in *Edinburgh Companion to Contemporary Scottish Literature*, ed. Berthold Schoene (Edinburgh: Edinburgh University Press, 2007), 29.

[11] Kaye Mitchell, *A.L. Kennedy* (Basingstoke: Palgrave Macmillan, 2008), 146.

[12] A.L. Kennedy, *What Becomes* (London: Jonathan Cape, 2009), 122.

[13] See, for example, Philip Tew, 'A New Sense of Reality? A New Sense of Text? Exploring Meta-Realism and the Literary-Critical Field', in *Beyond Postmodernism: Reassessment in Literature, Theory and Culture*, ed. Klaus Stierstorfer (Berlin and New York: Walter de Gruyer, 2003), 29-49.

[14] See Timotheus Velmeulen and Robin van den Akker, 'Notes on Metamodernism', *Journal of Aesthetics and Culture* 2 (2010), 1-14.

VICTOR SAGE

The Ambivalence of Laughter: the development of Nicola Barker's Grotesque Realism

> And we're bringing it along. We're getting all Dickensian again.
> All Rabelaisian, all 'how's yer father.'
> —Nicola Barker, *Clear*

Put your finger up to the spines and trace the point at which—just before Pat Barker—Nicola Barker's books begin to appear on the fiction shelves of the library or bookshop. Mark that almost hidden point, as the place where a discontinuity from the mainstream occurs. Her profile has been rising recently, but the nature of Barker's achievement does not seem any clearer to critics. Her last *London Review of Books* reviewer (like many readers before him) smells Dickens, and hints backhandedly that we may just have a great writer here in the making, but his uncertainty seems also very clear:

> Nicola Barker is Dickensian not so much because she is a maverick recorder or caricaturist of oddballs and grotesques, but because her sensibility is starkly oppositional: there are the bad guys (the middle classes) and the good (the marginal, but rich-in-life). She cares a lot. In eight novels she has never repeated herself: it may be that she's hardly started. If she can allow that hers is a talent that works better in a benign than a combative mood, then *Burley Cross Postbox Theft* may not be the throwaway it seems but the beginning of an expansion in a potentially great comic novelist.[1]

The 'Dickensian' label (even redefined as 'oppositional') needs a pinch of salt here: it is so often used to mask or promote 'eccentricity' and to shunt an author into a siding. Dickens's own reputation has not always been that of a great writer, and it seems here for James Lever, that all is still in the balance in Barker's work, unless she can relax her earnestness and give reign to her 'purely comic' genius. In a moment in which neo-realism (in Philip Hensher, say, and Jonathan Franzen) is making another bid for the centre ground, it might be worth having another look at the contours of Barker's work.

So far what we have is ten books: two collections of largely London-based short stories, *Love Your Enemies* (1993) and *Heading Inland* (1996), and a clutch of novels that have been steadily getting more ambitious. Classification has often used settings: we begin with the enigmatic working-class novel, set around a London betting-shop and dog-track, *Reversed Forecast* (1994), proceed to the beautifully-judged *Small Holdings* (1995), set in a North East London Park. After that, there's a leap in ambition and a move outside London to the first of what has been dubbed her 'Gateway Trilogy': the novel *Wide Open* (1998), which is set on the Isle of Sheppey and includes many aspects of the later novels' thematic content, but still retains the early style. Next comes *Five Miles From Outer Hope* (2000), a novel set in the Scilly Isles, which looks at first sight like a one-off, but I think is the breakthrough into the territory of her later grotesque hyperbolic style. Then the 2002 very demanding, but magnificent, continuation of the so-called trilogy: *Behindlings,* set this time on Canvey Island, again in the Thames Estuary. After that, an apparent diversion, a shorter and more occasional-looking work, *Clear* (2005), a 'transparent novel' as its disingenuous subtitle claims, a novel set back in London, based around the stunt of David Blaine, who had himself hoisted in a transparent cube above the Thames for 44 days without food and water. I say apparent diversion, because this novel, if judged by style and not setting, retains and develops the later style initiated in *Five Miles.* Finally, we have the formidable *Darkmans* (2007), set in the town of Ashford, Kent, a town which has become well-known as 'Ashford International', the last or first stop on Eurostar. But Barker's is an Ashford of a quite different kind, a medieval Ashford, lurking beneath the roundabouts and compulsory purchase orders of property for the new railway to Europe. This novel forms the climax of the trilogy of novels set in the 'Thames Gateway', and adds a layer of Gothic "darkness" to the parameters of the Grotesque. Beyond that, the most recent novel (2010) is a manic adventure in epistolary form, set in a Yorkshire village, *The Burley Cross Post-Office Theft*.

This corpus of work represents a startling achievement in fiction. One of the symptoms of the originality of the novels is that it is difficult to chart a way between one book and the next. Each book seems to set its own terms; texts are not easy to relate to each other. And yet there are strong thematic aspects of the early work from the 1990s, which follow on into the later, more challenging, more substantial books, and provide some tracks into this puzzling and disorientating territory. In what follows, I want briefly to examine the consistency of some of these thematic aspects of the early work, and to then relate them to features of style and the relationship with the reader in the later work.

The Grotesque Body: Some Contexts

Barker's work (and Dickens's work, too) is the product of a long tradition, which goes back to the pre-history of the novel genre in early parody and the "doubling" of high cultural forms in late Roman popular literature.[2] In the modernist context, Bakhtin's account of the discourse of this long tradition strikes an immediate chord with Joyce's comic interest in the relation between discourse and the body in *Ulysses*. For Barker's continued post-Joycean focus on the Grotesque Body, the most obvious source is Bakhtin's classic account of Rabelais.[3] The Grotesque is a style of representation, which insists, whatever the ostensible context, on the Body; and on what Bakhtin calls 'the material bodily lower stratum'. Its medium is parody; but Bakhtin maintains that this is a popular tradition in the medieval period. Not a tradition of intellectual satire, but a joyful and a utopian form of laughter which promotes 'free becoming'. He talks about how writers like Rabelais were not in thrall to such gloomy categories as 'eternity', but were freed by:

> . . . the gay and laughing aspect of the world, with its unfinished and open character, with the joy of change and renewal. This is why the medieval parodies were not formal and negative satires of sacred texts or of scholarly wisdom; they merely transposed these elements

into the key of gay laughter, into the positive material bodily sphere. Everything they touched was transformed into flesh and matter and at the same time was given a lighter tone (83).

And he quotes Rabelais' character Friar John who utters 'a Latin sentence characteristic of medieval grotesque': *Ad formam nasi cognoscitur ad te levavi*, 'by the shape of my nose you will know (how) I lift up', which is a parody of the Vulgate, Psalms 121, which the Protestant Bible knows as: 'I will lift up mine eyes unto the hills'. Clearly the old sexual joke about noses, penises and erections (Lat: *levare*), is used to debunk a sacred text; the exalted movement upwards in the rhetoric is converted to a movement down into the material sphere of the body, and so on.

Rabelais, insists Bakhtin, shows all the time that there is nothing in the sound and form of language that can escape the ambivalence created by this association with the body, and that this is what makes the grotesque into a form which celebrates freedom. And laughter of this kind, through its universality and freedom, had another important trait: its relation to 'the people's unofficial truth':

> The serious aspects of class culture are official and authoritarian; they are combined with violence, prohibitions, limitations and always contain an element of fear and intimidation. These elements prevailed in the Middle Ages. Laughter, on the contrary, overcomes fear, for it knows no inhibitions, no limitations. Its idiom is never used by violence and authority. (90)

Laughter is a victory not only 'over the mystic terror of God', but also over the awe inspired by the forces of nature and most of all over the oppression and guilt related to all that was consecrated and forbidden ("mana" and "taboo") (90). The 'defeat of fear' is presented in 'a droll and monstrous form', the symbols of power and violence turned inside out, the comic images of death and bodies gaily rent asunder. All that was terrifying becomes grotesque: Hell has burst and has poured forth abundance.

Bakhtin also suggests that historically, the eighteenth-century Enlightenment transferred the grotesque to a subjective sphere, which became what he calls the Romantic grotesque. Here, there is an overlap between the Gothic and the Grotesque. Unlike the Medieval and Renaissance grotesque, the genre acquired a private "chamber" character and was 'marked by a vivid sense of isolation' (37). He quotes the German *Sturm und Drang*, as a movement in which the Romantic grotesque is strong, and from this point on, fear is imported back into the grotesque: 'The images of the Romantic grotesque usually express fear of the world and seek to inspire their reader with this fear.' (38) It is the strength of Barker's grotesque that she is able to combine popular and intellectual traditions, retaining that traditional fearless, utopian drive in her images of bodily life.

Early Examples: Counting up Your World
Barker begins by writing about adolescents, or people in a state of incomplete consciousness of themselves, having been dominated by something two-dimensional which they have never questioned: a husband, or a friend or a set of rules and conventions. Many of these characters are female. Barker's first scenarios bring such characters to the point of consciousness, a point at which they ask the question, 'Where do I fit in?'

There is a scene in the novel *Small Holdings*,[4] in which the narrator, Phil, a twentysomething, still in the grip of a dreamy adolescent self-consciousness, tries to encompass the world he works in, a recently-privatised park in Palmers Green, North East London. Phil goes round the little universe he has been tending, seeking to eradicate the distance he feels from it, by enumerating in it all the things he has tended as a gardener, touching them intimately as he goes. But once he's finished enumerating the pond and the oaks, the flowerbeds and the greenhouses, he discovers there's no place for him. Phil is like a God who's invented the world, only to discover he has no place in it.

Phil is attempting this exercise in Zen because of a violent set of farcical events which have led to the death of Cog, the Park's resident ginger Tom and it has fallen to the hapless Phil to bury him. Suddenly, while contemplating his exclusion from his world, Phil sees Cog before him on the path. The cat, who has soil in his fur and thus is not a vision, immediately rolls on to his back and offers his belly for stroking and then 'saunters off, his jaunty little bollocks to the rear, and well-balanced like a sprig of cherries.' (80) This is the moment in which Phil suddenly decides to become someone else:

> Seeing the cat, like that, resurrected. It was so curious. Could I be someone else? Temporarily? Could I be someone else altogether? . . . Yes I could be. I could be un-Phil. Out-of-Phil. Un-fool-filled. Yes. (80)

It is the cat who carries the grotesque bodily charge of the resurrected body here, with the 'jaunty little bollocks', but it's Phil who takes the point: the Zen quest has been interrupted by an ethic of self-invention and the question 'Where do I fit in?' has been answered by Phil himself, out of Cog: 'anywhere you like.'

This revelation is the beginning of the end for the old Phil, not the end: there is a great deal of mayhem for out-of-Phil along the way, not least through his demonic one-legged mentor, Saleem, who delivers the novel's grotesque erotic climax in a remarkable sequence of denouement, which I have no space here to discuss.[5]

Barker's early grotesque takes many forms—the body is the focus, but the utopian challenge of self-invention is the scenario, in which the moment of liberation is set, a kind of 'gap' in people's lives, in which her characters suddenly think of themselves differently. Take the characters in *Love Your Enemies*,[6] her first book of stories. In the first story, 'Layla's Nose Job', Layla Carter has a nose two inches longer than anyone else's; the story details her agony and distress, in the way she's put upon by everybody, but also the way she puts upon herself. A therapist explains the castration complex, but it makes no difference. The eventual nose job makes no difference either, except it means things appear visually further away: she feels 'like Pinocchio' (11) after her father, Larry, says she's 'no longer his little elephant girl' (10); and dreams of being 'a tiny little elephant, but she was without a trunk.' (11) The story leaves her in the kitchen, having just accidentally sliced her egg to pieces, considering 'her options': which include, whether to castrate Larry, or cut the nose off altogether. Layla has entered the world.

Another scenario: Owen, an adolescent butcher's apprentice on a first day's work trial, is ritually mocked by his mentors, who persuade him a piece of meat is a living tumour. Owen believes them: he enters into an emotional ordeal smuggling the tumour home and nursing it all night, caring for it as it slowly dies and then secretly burying it in the garden. Next morning, when his mother asks him how his first day went, he says he's decided to become a postman. This is a deadpan joke, but it has the same structure: Owen, through the grotesque gate of the body has entered the world.

There is a grotesque aspect to events themselves in these stories; people suddenly manoeuvre themselves into spaces of change, crises, often through not knowing what they are doing. 'Skin', 'Food with Feeling', 'Symbiosis: Class Cestoda', and 'Country Matters' are all based around this kind of scenario. Even private fictions about the body, like the tumour, are taken for granted as necessities. Farce is an aspect of the collection's grotesque, often involving the body. Take 'Dual Balls' for example, a story of female friendship in the culturally barren 'Grunty Fen' in remote Cambridgeshire, in which her 'dominant and rather light-headed friend' (95), Joanna, is 'the bale of hay in Selina's field' (96), which would otherwise remain featureless, so impeccable is the hardworking schoolteacher's life. In a conspiracy with her (in turn) dominant husband Tom, Joanna dares Selina to conduct a class at the primary school with a mailorder battery-driven sex-toy inside her. What Joanna, having tried them out and almost driven off the road, doesn't tell Tom, who assumes they are useless, is that the dual balls of the title actually do have remarkable powerful sexual effects. Nervously, Selina puts them in and switches them on in the toilets. During the short walk to her classroom 'the balls felt like an inordinately large bluebottle whizzing round, lost inside her knickers.' (109) As planned, the children have not arrived, but lo and behold, the headmistress, Felicity, is there, sitting in the front row, wanting a discussion about Selina's career. A series of farcical misunderstandings follow, in which the strict and severely proper Selina's involuntary orgasm is interpreted by the headmistress as a gush of genuine passion about her career, and Felicity resolves to promote her as her successor. Even here, the forces of ignorance and convention are the means by which the frustratedly ambitious but unconfident Selina, by accepting the risk of a joke on her that backfires, invents a new future for herself. This story is part of a continuous, post-feminist parody of identity politics, which is taken for granted throughout these stories.

The discursive frame of these early comic scenarios is witty and sharp, but confines itself to the reportage of events, essentially using grotesque farce as an entrance to 'free becoming'. Remaining for a moment on the level of style, in my view, the "break-through" text is not *Wide Open*, the first of the Gateway trilogy written in 1998, but the lesser novel, *Five Miles From Outer Hope* (2000). In many ways, *Wide Open* is bursting out of its own narrative discourse. Dealing with a question inherited from Ionesco, that of whether two people can live the same life in separate bodies, that novel deliberately (and experimentally) puts maximum strain on the methods of reportage and the grotesquerie of events of the early phase I've been talking about.[7] The utopian drive towards freedom of the traditional Grotesque, which her early work has succeeded in tapping into so consistently, combined with Barker's interest in mysticism, already manifest in the Zen undercurrent (bookended in epigraphs from Shan-hui and Lieh-tzu) of *Small Holdings*, are reflected in the title of this extraordinary novel, *Wide Open*, which follows the tradition of 'Bakhtin's 'double body' of the grotesque, in which the body is open to the cosmos.[8]

But I have no space to demonstrate this point. Instead, let me give a retrospective glimpse of the Barkerian future, let me quote a typical passage from the discourse of Medve, the doughty "giantess" and first-person narrator of *Five Miles*,[9] who constructs herself (in her 1981 mode) before our very eyes:

> Medve is Hungarian for bear, which, when you think about it, is pretty fucking grizzly. And don't ask me how to pronounce it. I will inflate and then I will gently burst. And it will be messy, because I am built like a shire horse. Six foot three in my crocheted stockings. I am *huge*. Sixteen years old in 1981, with a tongue taut and twisted as a tent-hook and two tremendous hands like flat meat racquets.
> *Thwack!*
> My serve, I think. (7)

Medve uses the stand-up comic's routine addiction to stress, a kind of mime in language, which will eventually yield diminishing returns. But hers is expanded polyphonic narration, fully dialogic, fully obscene, fully billingsgate, as Bakhtin would say, in which the reader is facing the narrator as a nightmare opponent across a tennis net, an analogy for dialogue famously used by both Beckett and Nabokov and knowingly reprised here. We are looking here at the future character of Barker's narration: and, from here on in, it is no longer going to be well-behaved:

> My clitoris, you'll be pleased to know, is as well-defined as the rest of me. It's the approximate size of a Jersey Royal. But whenever I try and *mash* it (don't *sweat*, I know these particular potatoes are determined *boilers,* but *flow* with the analogy, for once, why don't you?), all I can think about is Mr Michael Heseltine MP eating an overripe peach on a missile site somewhere deep in the South Downs—or the general vicinity— juice on his tie, shit on his shoes. Am I ringing a bell? Do you think this might *mean* something? (13)

Medve's italics are to pepper the novels to come, and pretty soon they will also be used to signify the simultaneous presence of a stream of consciousness, embedded in the roman of a third-person discourse, a process in which thinking is often deliberately opposed to speaking so that the same person is thinking "dog" and saying "cat". The discourse itself has become hyperbolic, its texture is formally grotesque: Medve, in her callow dependency on the despised opponent, the reader, produces a finely-contrived collapse in the ambivalence between neediness and defiance in her last question ('Do you think this might *mean* something?') and manufactures an excess of language, varnished with anxious (encyclopaedic[10]) pedantry and adolescent contempt. She is just the beginning of a textual expansion into fictional self-consciousness which is neither realist nor post-modern, but which treats the mouth as the centre of the grotesque body and the baroque quicksilver of the speaking voice as its major symptom.

[1] James Lever, 'Unshutuppable', *London Review of Books*, September 9, 2010, 27.

[2] See M. M. Bakhtin, 'From the Pre-History of Novelistic Discourse', in T*he Dialogic Imagination*, ed. Michael Holquist, trans. Caryl Emerson and Michael Holquist (Austin and London: University of Texas Press, 1981), 41-84.

[3] All references to M. M. Bakhtin, *Rabelais and His World*, trans. Helene Iswolsky, (Cambridge and London: MIT Press, 1968). Quotations followed by page refs in text.

[4] All references to Nicola Barker, *Small Holdings* (London: Faber, 1995).

[5] But which the reader will find on pp.109-112.

[6] Nicola Barker, *Love Your Enemies* (London: Faber, 1993). All references to this edition.

[7] Nicola Barker, *Wide Open* (London: Faber, 1998), 8. This question haunts the opening chapters by the 'Two Ronnies'. The tone of the dialogue is not celebratory, but baffled and opaque:

> ' . . . You said you knew someone in Sheppey.'
>
> 'You.'
>
> Ronnie frowned. 'What ?'
>
> 'You're the person I know in Sheppey.'
>
> 'But we only just met.'
>
> The other Ronnie cleared his throat. 'Same people', he said, 'different lives.' (32)

[8] The title plays on 'wide open spaces' (e.g. the skies of Sheppey) and the vulnerability of a person turned towards them, opening their bodies (and thus souls): 'And he simply hadn't felt right with Laura after that. In fact, he felt wide open. A moth with its wings pinned, under the microscope. A girl with her legs spread, no knickers.' Nicola Barker, *Wide Open* (London: Faber, 2008), 61. The character is vulnerable; but at the same time the lens of the organism is opened to its widest extent. Compare the following passage from Bakhtin: '[The grotesque . . .] is looking for that which protrudes from the body, all that seeks to go out beyond the body's confines . . . But the most important of all human features for the grotesque is actually reduced to the gaping mouth . . . the other features are only a frame encasing this wide-open bodily abyss.'

Bakhtin, *Rabelais*, 316.

[9] All references to Nicola Barker, *Five Miles From Outer Hope* (London: Faber, 2000).

[10] For some comment on the encyclopaedism of Rabelais, see Bakhtin, *Rabelais*, 110.

CHINA MIÉVILLE

5 to Read

The usual caveats obtain: any list of "favourite", "best", "most interesting", "most overlooked", any list at all can only ever be a fraught and freighted frozen moment, subject to any instant's revision and hedged around with whatabouts. Yesterday this might have comprised five other names; tomorrow it might comprise five other again.

Underknownness is here the key. Even among new and newish and young and youngish writers, a ruthless maximum celebrity must be enforced. Helen Oyeyemi, for example, is a magnificent young British writer, but having been justly feted, recent recipient of a Somerset Maugham Award, she is not here. Of course, inclusion here is no guarantee of on-going anonymity: indeed, the opposite is to be hoped.

All lists are acts of canonisation, and a list organised around neglect and/ or insufficient notice must be one of counter-canonisation. All moments in literature create their own foundations. When new generations stand upon those shoulders, this piece will be more than an exercise in nostalgia.

It is perhaps obvious to say, but worth pointing out nonetheless, that here we proceed from the position that in literature, honourable failure is vastly preferable to dishonourable success, high-risk aesthetic aspiration (even with, sometimes, concomitant inadequacies) to flawless safety. There may very well, then, be various things wrong—sometimes obviously or very wrong—with some of the works listed here. Not only does that not matter, but if that wrongness comes in the service of a reaching, the sense, to borrow a metaphor from Jeffrey Ford, of an inchworm at the end of a branch, stretching and repeatedly groping for something beyond, then it may even be something to celebrate.

Marion Fox (1885–1973)

One of the quirks of lovers of the fantastic is their—our—simultaneously charming and infuriating lack of discrimination, according to which *any* book with *anything* fantastic in it is more or less as voraciously consumed as any other. Sometimes we lack a sense that while *this* book was one we thoroughly enjoyed, it might not be suitable for a civilian who does not share our pulp and/or macabre predilections. Whereas this *other* one is a major work by any standards, and its low profile a literary crime.

So *Ape's-Face*. Once a well-received writer, who produced several works of fiction between 1910 and 1928, Marion Fox lay utterly obscure until 2006, when the estimable small press Ash-Tree Press released the novel for which she is listed here, *Ape's-Face* (1914). The book is perhaps too odd to ever quite be a classic, but in any sane literary firmament it would count as a major mooncalf anticlassic.

The story itself is of the transference—inevitable, just, unjust, by manipulation and guile, whatever—of property; of secret affairs; of manifestations of *things* in landscape; of the resurgence of the past; of an ancestral curse, a monster, that stalks a family, and places this within the "weird" tradition, though it has been neglected even in that neglected corner. With its obsession with a returned, inadequately repressed fratricidal violence, the book's publication at the start of the First World War feels like no coincidence.

What raises Fox's piece above the level of an enjoyable bagatelle is the complex of psychological and formal peculiarities that distinguish it. Her calm and homely heroine, whose cruel nickname gives the book its title, has something of Jane Eyre about her, but within the context of a class-mobile family shot through with early twentieth-century angst about that very mobility.

The writing itself veers between registers, in a kind of ingenuous avant-garde, vaguely reminiscent of Barbara Comyns at times; more, though the fit is still imprecise, of Mary Butts. Fox's experimentation is, though—seemingly at least—less deliberate than Butts's, a more naive and occasional modernism of, at times, astonishing strangeness. In her fascination with inanimate things' interactions without humans, for example, Fox prefigures the *au courant* trendy concerns of "object-oriented philosophy". This is the case above all in Chapter VI, 'Strange Conversation between Two Chairs'.

By the time the ancient evil manifests, towards the book's end, it is barely the weirdest thing we have encountered.

William Hope Hodgson (1877–1917)

"Weird fiction", that slippery anti-gothic macabre that reached its high point in the early years of the twentieth century, is receiving more and more sustained scholarly and cultural attention than it ever has before. What was for decades almost exclusively a marginal concern for specialists and enthusiasts, has become or is becoming of interest to some among the literati.

This is most evident in the growing attention to the work of H. P. Lovecraft, the key figure in this para-canon. In the last few years his pulp-modernist work has been the subject of an important study by Michel Houellebecq, translated by the hip US imprint McSweeneys, and has been brought out by such respectable imprints as the Library of America and Penguin Classics. Where Lovecraft is vanguard, others have followed: Penguin also now publishes the work of Algernon Blackwood, for example.

One figure still unendorsed by such propriety, though he has long been a favourite among the horror geekoscenti, is William Hope Hodgson. An amazing polymath, a pioneering photographer and body-builder, Hodgson was also a poet and author of an extraordinary and voluminous series of prose works. Ranging from horrifying sea stories (pioneering in their cephalopod-focus), through vigorous Edwardian psychic-detectiviana (*Carnacki the Ghost-Finder* [1910–12]), to works of deeply flawed but floorlessly deep ecstatic vision, like *The House on the Borderland* (1908) and, above all, his at times excruciatingly cack-handed but utterly searing apocalypse dream *The Night-Land* (1912).

Hodgson died at the Western Front, and his correspondence from that charnel zone makes clear and explicit the connections between the bad numinous of weird fiction, its obsessive focus on formless monstrosities and, to use Hodgson's own preferred formulation, *abhuman* landscapes, and the epochal enormity of the First World War. That Hodgson's writing taps this vein without slipping into the ostentatious reactionary ecstasy of Lovecraft or Arthur Machen makes it all the more important. Hodgson's single greatest work is a story of the war itself—published, poignantly, shortly after his death. 'Eloi, Eloi, Lama Sabachthani', is a neglected classic of First World War literature, a key text, deserving of a place alongside the poetry of Owen, Rosenberg and Sassoon. An irruption of humane yet visionary terror overwhelms what starts as relatively workmanlike prose, until the text invokes 'some Christ-aping monster of the void'. A ghastly implication is not stated, but hangs there: that there is no aping at all, that this monster is the deity that allows the Somme.

Jane Gaskell (1941–)

Gaskell, like Oyeyemi, was the winner of a Somerset Maugham Award. Unlike Oyeyemi, unfortunately, that she remains underknown seems unarguable.

Perhaps the variety of Gaskell's output, one of the very qualities that make her oeuvre so fascinating, has counted against her. Highly schematically, her work clusters around two centres of gravity: on the one hand, strange and dreamlike fantasies set in fraught fairylands or violent lost continents (*Strange Evil* [1957]; the *Atlan* series [1963–1977]; *King's Daughter* [1958]); on the other, wry, sometimes cruel, meticulously observed London lives (*All Neat in Black Stockings* [1968]; *Attic Summer* [1969]; *Summer Coming* [1972]; *Sun Bubble* [1990]).

In fact what is key to the schema is not only Gaskell's range (and precocity—her first novel, *Strange Evil*, a sultry and violent fairytale, was written when she was fourteen) but the extent to which the distinction between her 'fantasy' and her 'realism', is, in fact, unstable. Gaskell's ultra-rare and excellent vampire novel, *The Shiny Narrow Grin* (1964), for example, is as much an unsentimental observation of youth culture and psychodramas as it is about the undead. *Summer Coming*, amid its realistic depictions of London sex and angst, features one abrupt and jarring moment of the seemingly supernatural that is barely remarked upon by the characters. Even her last book, *Sun Bubble*, a strangely structured but wholly 'realist' work about a single mother struggling to make a way in London, through wince-making familial cruelty and painfully convincing emotional failings, feels like a dream. It is structured by a disobedient sense of time, a passionate and oneiric intensity that makes it feel as if the impossible might occur at any moment.

Perhaps Gaskell's key work is the one for which she won the Somerset Maugham Award, *A Sweet, Sweet Summer* (1969), precisely because it is in equipoise between these two poles. It is not realist at all, being set in a London successfully invaded by aliens that hang over the city in impossible ships. But those overlords (which order the public execution of Ringo Starr) remain ostentatiously out of sight, and their reign is characterised by a vivid and catastrophic heightening of pre-existing and real tensions within youth and sub-cultures, of everyday prejudices, violence, and longings. This is a post-apocalypse narrative of a very strange sort, the apocalypse being as much one of longing, incompetent emotion and overwrought London-ness as of extra-terrestrial despotism and the ruins of war. The omission of this extraordinary work from the various regularly compiled lists of "visionary London writing" is unforgivable.

Lavie Tidhar (1976–)
Tidhar is a prolific young Israeli writer, resident in London, and considered part of the British scene here. In fact his varied work, reflecting the many places he has chosen to live, is characterised by a restless cosmopolitanism. Claiming it as British is, then, while not wholly unreasonable, a tendentious and political intervention into what Britishness-in-fiction can, could, should be, and can never foreclose all the other things his fiction is.

His commitment to internationalism and quality in speculative/science fiction is evident in his editorship of the two volumes of *The Apex Book of World SF* (2009, 2012) and stewardship of the World SF blog (http://worldsf. wordpress.com); the carefully varied cultural settings of his fiction, sometimes meticulously specific and carefully drawn (*The Tel Aviv Dossier*, with Nir Yaniv [2009]), sometimes cheerfully syncretic (*Jesus and the Eightfold Path* [2011]); and his committed interventions in the debates around the ethnic and national exclusivity of much of the (science-fictional/fantastic) imaginary. He is a political writer, an iconoclast and sometimes a provocateur, whose provocations are for specific ends and generally against a reactionary given, rather than being a pointless or recursive game.

Tidhar has been a prolific writer of short fiction—a form considerably more vibrant and celebrated in the fantastic genres than in "mainstream" literature—and novellas. What has recently brought him increasing notice is his novel *Osama* (2011), for which he was shortlisted for various awards.

The book is a fine and elegant many-worlds riff, a melancholy noir rumination, an alternative world story (of sorts) in which Osama Bin Laden is a character in the action stories of a mysterious pulp writer. From that conceit the plot becomes a conspiracy thriller (of sorts), an angry political novel (of sorts), a post-9/11 elegy (of sorts, and without mawkishness). It is a remarkable and ambitious work, that strives, abjuring the nostalgia and self-congratulation of the sf field at its worst, to use the tools of the fantastic/science-fictional to extract fuel for thought from what might have felt an exhausted seam.

I. Hips (1979–)

Hips has claimed variously that the initial 'I' stands for 'Indira', 'Iain' and 'Io'. As Hips does not appear in public or give face-to-face or phone interviews, her/his gender is unknown. It is known that s/he was born in 1978 in London, and the city features in much of her/his work. Hips has insisted in an interview with *3:AM Magazine* that s/he regularly appears at public events, but simply prefers not to announce her/himself. (In 2008, a rumour circulated that the fourth novel in the *Kill-Burn* series, *Goading the Sea-Scouts*, was to be longlisted for the Orange Prize, if the author would verify that s/he was female.)

Hips's first and second books were non-fiction. 2001's *Before the Rooster Crows: A History in Disavowed Books*, a precocious, millennia-spanning study of works repudiated by their authors. In it Hips not only provocatively insists that various curios are their authors' central works (eccentrically privileging

Ballard's *The Wind from Nowhere* over *The Atrocity Exhibition*, for example), but formulates a theory in which what the author calls 'the outcast book' is the key heuristic for decoding human civilisation. A second edition was released in 2011, excising a rather heavy-handed chapter insisting that the Bible was disavowed by God, and replacing it with a consideration of Jonathan Littell's *Bad Voltage*.

Hips's second book, *Orpheus and the Bad Trains* (2004), was a long photographic essay about those stretches of the London Underground network where the trains emerge from tunnels and travel uncovered tracks. Since then, Hips has entered a period of great productivity, publishing epic poetry (*I Hide (In Plain Sight)* [2006]), children's books (*Corvidious* [2006], *The Angry Tweezers* [2008]), and the series of short, very loosely related novels set in northwest London known as *The Kill-Burn Cycle* (2005–ongoing). It is with these last books that Hips is building something of a following.

So far there are six *Kill-Burn* books: *Go In Gwynne* (2005); *Goading the Sea Scouts* (2007); *The Rage of Trees* (2008); *I Come to Sew Your Lips to This* (2008); *Magnets and Cars* (2009); and *Canary in the Brick Mine* (2011).

Varying wildly in tone, from the rumbustiously Dickensian and cheerfully filthy *Go In Gwynne*, through unremitting Barkerian body-horror (*I Come . . .*), the *Kill-Burn* novels transmogrify the city into a landscape of friendly and unfriendly grotesques, political eschatology and commodified dreaming. Whatever their register, they are exuberant and giddying state-of-the-nation ruminations, and indispensable to any consideration of the modern British novel.

BERTHOLD SCHOENE

Cosmo-Kitsch vs. Cosmopoetics

Critics continue to appraise the British novel for its capacity to imagine the nation. Patrick Parrinder concludes *Nation and Novel* with the assertion that 'twenty-first-century novelists will continue to participate in the making and remaking of English identity',[1] while Bruce King seems to be contradicting the title of his book *The Internationalization of English Literature* when he suggests that what we are currently witnessing is the writing of 'a new national literature'.[2] My own interest is in disclosing trends in contemporary British literary practice that explore twenty-first-century life outside such national-ist paradigms and go beyond imagining the world in terms of an irresolvable vying for predominance between globalising centres and globalised peripher-ies, which appears to be informing both imperialist and post-colonial writing. My basic contention is that twenty-first-century globalisation has resulted in paradigm-shifting change not only for the life of the nation, but also for its representation. As I will show, at its clumsiest, least convincing yet also most popular, the new cosmopolitan writing is not really cosmopolitan at all, but consigns our fractured, closely interconnected life-world to the same hierar-chies that have governed peoples' lives for centuries while paying lip service to the world's potential as a global village in continual convivial flux. At its best, by contrast, the new cosmopolitan novel deconstructs the extant hege-monies by engaging in a cosmopoetic recasting of our ever-increasingly glo-balised condition. In other words, the very form and texture of the realist novel undergo significant transformation as its generic aesthetics must rise to the challenge of imagining humanity in its planetary entirety.

As Brian Finney points out, British fiction is now being produced in response to 'a world which is so thoroughly interconnected that it is no longer possible to treat any part of it as unaffected by everything else'.[3] Indeed increasing globalisation has seen the rise of a new kind of middlebrow fiction, which mobilises the wretchedness of illegal immigrants, asylum-seekers, and victims of human trafficking ostensibly for the purpose of popular consciousness-raising. Yet its true motivation is exonerative; it is primarily designed to exorcise British middle-class guilt accrued by leading irresponsible, unsustainable lives and giving in to varying degrees of world-political fatigue and disengagement. It is this new genre that I designate as 'cosmo-kitsch'. Orbiting the West's ethical failure, cosmo-kitsch novels diligently research the viewpoint and voice of the often severely traumatised other so that the would-be cosmopolitan writer can tell his subject's tale and speak on her behalf, confident that his impeccable intentions will outweigh any charges of exploitative appropriation. Cosmo-kitsch novels frequently culminate in grand reconciliatory visions of transnational human fellowship engineered to demonstrate that the other's exposure and helplessness, if perhaps not her bare-life precarity, are in fact shared by us all. This is, then, not cosmopolitan literature at all; rather than written about, or to, the world, these texts constitute strictly ethnocentric middle-class monologues nursing a primarily western quandary. Oscillating between self-pity and self-congratulation, their ultimate aim is to beat home the fundamental entitlement of British middle-class folks to a good life unencumbered by guilt.

One best-selling proponent of cosmo-kitsch is Chris Cleave's *The Other Hand*.[4] In Cleave's novel the editor of a women's magazine accepts the freebie of a beach holiday in Nigeria in the hope of reconnecting with her estranged husband, a left-leaning political journalist. Once in Nigeria the couple ignore all local advice, stroll out of their heavily-guarded compound, and immediately get caught up in a group of bandits threatening two teenage girls, sole survivors of a village massacre nearby. The bandits offer the couple a chance to save the girls' lives in exchange for one of their fingers each; only the editor steps up to this gruesome challenge, thus saving the younger sister (who goes by the name of 'Little Bee'). On their return to London, unable to cope with his guilt and shame, the husband lapses into deep depression and eventually hangs himself as Little Bee turns up on the couple's doorstep, following her arrival in Britain as a stowaway. Even though it contrasts the pampered lives of middle-class Londoners with people's desperate struggle for survival in a conflict-ridden "Third World" most effectively, Cleave's novel also bears many unforgivable shortcomings. Not only does Cleave have a penchant for spelling out the self-evident, as in the editor's lover's admission to Little Bee that 'you're the brave little refugee girl, and I'm the selfish bastard' (269), the novel is saturated with clichéd stereotyping regarding the African point of view, and Little Bee seems infantilised by her very name, an effect worsened by her revelation that 'Little Bee is only my superhero name' (313). Most worrying, though, is the language assigned to her by Cleave. Cleave's assurance in the appendix that he worked hard to get this particular aspect of the novel absolutely right appears implausible when read alongside exoticising imagery like 'she was whispering [. . .] in some language that sounded like butterflies drowning in honey' (19).

Nestling within the cosmopolitan cliché of London as 'a world of its own, a country within a country' (1), Amanda Craig's *Hearts and Minds*,[5] which summons a broad mix of international characters (from the US to Zimbabwe and the Ukraine) represents another exemplar of cosmo-kitsch writing. Despite efforts to share the novel's limelight equally among all its characters, the plot continues to revolve around Polly Noble, a human rights lawyer, whose nanny Iryna, an illegal Russian immigrant, has been found murdered in the city. Polly and Iryna are joined on the have-not side of the novel's global citizenry by Anna, a trafficked teenage prostitute from the Ukraine, and Job, a Zimbabwean asylum seeker, and on the side of the haves by Ian, a 'freewheeling' (13) ex-pat Australian teacher, and his South African fiancée, as well as US American Katie, who gets sucked into 'the kind of thing that somebody from her world [n]ever has to deal with' (288), namely her next-door neighbour Anna's life-or-death escape from her captors. Despite the blatant discrepancies among its cast, Craig's novel never misses an opportunity to invoke a sense of communal fellowship among her characters, insisting that 'there is no us and them. There's just *people*. We're all migrants from somewhere' (199). Craig's perhaps most facile and cloying manoeuvre in this context is her portrayal of Iryna as 'like so many Londoners, a person who did not fit in anywhere else, and who had come to the city hoping to find a new beginning' (3), quite as if the identity of "Londoner" were ever acquired so easily by an illegal immigrant. In Craig's novel London is introduced to us as a neoliberal utopia, ideal for free-spirited, independent-minded individuals whose determination and eccentricity identifies them as members of one and the same quasi-national community, irrespective of their vastly divergent points of departure. *Hearts and Minds* engages in glib cosmopolitan myth-making. Dialogic narration is offered as an antidote to political disenfranchisement, while living in London is suggested in and of itself to elide categorical segregation by nationality and economic caste. Finally, we are reassured that, however appalling racism and exploitation in the UK may be, never do they quite compare to the US American outlook, which in Craig's novel is represented by Polly's ex-husband: 'By "people", Theo always means those like himself, who earn a minimum of a million pounds a year; the rest do not exist' (6).

The problem with both Cleave and Craig is the presumptuousness of their cosmopolitan ventriloquism, their monologic speaking for the underprivileged and disenfranchised, whose primary objective is so clearly not a critique of globalisation but the alleviation of British middle-class guilt. Like *The Other Hand*, Craig's novel is not without its commendable highlights. The ongoing Western Orientalisation of the "Third World", and Africa in particular, is aptly captured in Job's remark that 'few people make the distinction between one African country and another' (24), while casual stereotypes of Africa as culturally inferior or, indeed, as uncivilised abound. Looking at a child's map of the world, Job finds that 'over Zimbabwe there is only the figure of a rhinoceros' (339). But at the same time *Hearts and Minds* is guilty of its own awkward animal imagery: London's wild flocks of bright green parakeets are described as 'teasing the heavy, predatory crows in much the same way that the Bangladeshi boys at [Ian's] school do the Afro-Caribbeans' (18). Perhaps most revealing of the brittleness of Craig's cosmopolitan outlook, however, is her move to highlight Job's moral entitlement to British residency by showing him selflessly pre-empt an Islamist suicide attack. Is such a heroic feat really the only means available to Craig to reassure her readership of the globalised other's civic worth? Ironically, it takes the murder of her Russian nanny for Polly herself to get anywhere near fulfilling the promise of her familial heritage ('Noble'), and even then pathos and self-pity prevail: 'Shame scalds [Polly]', we are told, when she realises she has been exploiting Iryna without a thought for 'that young woman's own personality or needs' (285). Imagining Western encounters with Third World precarity, both *The Other Hand* and *Hearts and Minds* pose one of cosmopolitanism's most fundamental questions, namely 'what does [one] owe a total stranger' (290)? Yet the answer to this question remains veiled and mired in melodrama.

Unlike Cleave's and Craig's, the novels of David Mitchell and Hari Kunzru are informed by an understanding that imagining global community and giving voice to a new cosmopolitical ethics challenges the realist novel not only thematically, but moreover tests its fundamental cosmopoetic capability, involving alongside plot and characterisation globality's very dimensionality of time and space. However multicultural and international in scope, Craig's and Cleave's novels remain focalised through the ethnocentric lens of the nation, whereas Mitchell—whose *Ghostwritten* and *Cloud Atlas* set an entirely new standard for cosmopolitan writing[6]—elicits a sense of global cohesion precisely by yielding to the world's brokenness and fragmentation, a sense of global connectivity and neighbourly proximity by representing individual alienation, and a sense of world community by envisioning humanity beyond any determinate purpose other than reiterating the fundamental condition of our planetary conviviality. The understanding that everybody else is in the world with us and therefore deserves our attention and compassion transcends the globe's internationalist compartmentalisation. Cosmopoetics, then, thrives not on constellations of self-contained characters unmistakably told apart by passport, but on what Homi Bhabha has described as the proliferation of 'continua of identification'[7] unfurling from the synchronicity of people's lives, their globalised being-in-common. As a closer look reveals, *Hearts and Minds* is not actually so very far removed from a cosmopoetic view that would portray Polly *as* Katie *as* Anna, seemingly emerging from parallel worlds that are indeed always one and the same world, or Ian the (Australian) teacher *as* Job the (Zimbabwean) teacher, one of whom is permitted to practise in London while the other is not.

The correspondences between Hari Kunzru's cosmopolitan vision in *Gods without Men*[8] and Mitchell's in *Cloud Atlas* are conspicuous. In both texts the characters come in constellations that are open cosmopoetic paradigms, anticipating and seemingly replicating one another, each individual existence reverberating with the life-stories of a multitude of contemporaries, ancestors and descendants. Like all biometrical detail, identity descriptors such as nationality and religion blur and refract in the heat of the Californian desert, where Kunzru's novel is set, and so too does the seemingly fixed frame of the contemporary as time itself begins to open wide, facilitating a strong sense of affinity between lives lived in times immemorial: the 1770s, the 1870s, various decades of the twentieth century, as well as the immediate present of 2008/9. Kunzru's novel amalgamates Native American myth, the diary of an eighteenth-century Spanish missionary, the communal records of a 1960s extraterrestrial worshipping cult, contemporary pop and celebrity culture, as well as the media frenzy surrounding the mystery of a vanished child, thus reflecting the vision of *Cloud Atlas* which presents humanity, and the repertory of stories that make up our history, as invariably the same but different. According to *Gods without Men*, 'there had been not one but sixteen crucified saviours since the dawn of time, and most of the Bible was copied from ancient Irish druids' (63). Denying themselves the teleology of neat narrative progress or the comfort of a proper ending, Mitchell and Kunzru consign their novels to desultory patterns of recurrence and recommencement. As Mitchell puts it in *Cloud Atlas*, their ambition is nothing less than to capture the universals of the human condition, the creation of 'a never-changing map of the ever constant ineffable' (389). As Slavoj Žižek has explained, it is crucial to understand such invocations of eternity 'not in the sense of a series of abstract-universal features that may be applied everywhere, but in the sense that [the truth] has to be re-invented in each new historical situation'.[9] Accordingly, by invoking in conclusion 'certain mysteries concerning life and death, which as soon as they had been revealed receded into forgetfulness, for that which is infinite is known only to itself and cannot be contained in the mind of man' (384), Kunzru hints at a divine world-truth that unravels as it announces itself, leaving us with no viable access to the meaning of human existence other than our own evanescent, inevitably contracted contemporary lives.

At its most contemporary level *Gods without Men* tells the story of the Matharus, a Sikh-Jewish American couple, whose autistic four-year-old son Raj disappears in the Californian desert. There are insinuations that what may have occurred is an alien abduction, yet far more compelling is the suggestion that Raj never actually leaves Pinnacle Rocks, but that he is lost in time. His location remains the same while he is transported to different moments in time, which is precisely how his disappearance comes to rivet the novel's manifold temporal plates. Visiting Pinnacle Rocks in the 1920s, an ethnographer sees 'an Indian walking hand in hand with a white child, a boy of about five years of age' (215), and Judy, a girl that disappeared in the same spot in the 1960s, is said to have left with 'the glow boy' (67), who may or may not have been Raj. Raj's vanishing, time-travel, and miraculous return accentuate the novel's interrogation of the very substantiality of modern individuality, holding it up to the cosmopoetics of Bhabha's 'continua of identification'. 'Every moment is a bardo', the novel suggests, 'suspended between past and future. We are always in transition, slipping from one state to the next', thereby causing individuality in the end to amount to little more than 'just a momentary confluence of forces' (351). In this light, the interracial union of Jaz and Lisa, Raj's parents, which results in the birth of a special child 'belonging half to this world and half to the Land of the Dead' (129), appears as both a repeat and fulfilment of the equally frowned-upon union of Mockingbird Runner and Eliza Deighton almost a hundred years previously. *Gods without Men* shows the world to coincide in cosmopolitan simultaneity, always to be interconnected both spatially and temporally, which leads to startling instances of cosmopoetic envisioning in the post-9/11 Californian desert:

Heat haze splashed mirages across the highway and for a moment

Jaz wasn't sure if the thing he saw was real: a group of women walking by the roadside, swathed in sky-blue Afghan burqas. It was as if a shard of television had fallen into his eyes, a stray image from elsewhere. He slowed and checked his mirrors. There they were, incomprehensible cobalt ghosts, making their way from one place to another. (94)

Lisa's subsequent glimpse of 'two women in head-to-toe Muslim tents' accompanied by a teenage boy 'in jeans and T-shirt, carrying a skateboard' (114) confirms Jaz's vision as an actual sighting: these Californian Muslim women are simultaneously Afghan aliens and first-generation Americans, dislocated anachronistic chimeras and real, authentic manifestations of our immediate here and now.

The boldness of Kunru's novel shows in his choice of America, the great global homogeniser and hegemon, as the setting for his cosmopolitan text. Implementing cosmopoetic devices pioneered by Mitchell, Kunzru provides an x-ray of the human condition, disclosing the contemporary not so much as the uppermost layer in an historical palimpsest as in itself palimpsestic, transfused by Native American myth, Catholic mysticism, faith in extraterrestrials, and so forth, including Jaz's economic algorithmics and suppressed Sikhism, as well as Lisa's post-traumatic return to Judaism. Kunzru dismantles the clichéd vision of our Americanized Brave New World as 'full of people who looked as if they'd just been unwrapped from their packaging, all shiny and expensive, like audio equipment. People who came with curls of foam and polythene bags and cable ties' (17). *Gods without Men* appears to be saying that while twenty-first-century humanity may indeed resemble a brand-new series of gadgets of a specific, hitherto unprecedented kind, they find themselves invariably slotted into one and the same old inscrutable kaleidoscope of a world, which is our world.

NOTES

[1] Patrick Parrinder, *Nation and Novel: The English Novel from Its Origins to the Present Day* (Oxford: Oxford University Press, 2006), 414.

[2] Bruce King, *The Internationalization of English Literature* (Oxford: Oxford University Press, 2004), 324.

[3] Brian Finney, *English Fiction Since 1984: Narrating a Nation* (New York: Palgrave, 2006), 2.

[4] Chris Cleave, *The Other Hand* (London: Hodder & Stoughton, 2008).

[5] Amanda Craig, *Hearts and Minds* (London: Little Brown, 2009).

[6] David Mitchell, *Ghostwritten: A Novel in Nine Parts* (London: Sceptre, 1999) and *Cloud Atlas* (London: Sceptre, 2004).

[7] Homi Bhabha, 'Unpacking My Library … Again', in *The Post-Colonial Question: Common Skies, Divided Horizons*, ed. by Iain Chambers and Lidia Curti (London: Routledge, 1996), 203.

[8] Hari Kunzru, *Gods without Men* (London: Hamish Hamilton, 2011).

[9] Slavoj Žižek, *First as Tragedy, Then as Farce* (London: Verso, 2009), 6.

ANDREW CRUMEY

Teaching Creative Writing

The basic lesson on how to become a writer has been put well enough by Stephen King: you've got to read a lot and write a lot.[1] This is how writers have done it throughout history, though there is also abundant evidence of writers having made use of informal networks and support groups to help them along. Flaubert read the whole of *The Temptation of Saint Antony* to two friends who listened patiently then advised him to put it on the fire and write something else (he came up with *Madame Bovary*). *Frankenstein* emerged from what might nowadays be called a workshop, when Byron, Polidori and the Shelleys set themselves the task of writing a horror story.

Some writers may prefer to work in isolation, but for many the most important early step is finding others willing to give an opinion, and it is this basic function that is served by the creative writing group, whether it is an informal meeting of friends or a professionally run activity. My own start as a novelist was through attending creative writing classes in England run by the Workers' Education Association, which followed the standard workshop format where participants took turns to read their work aloud for subsequent group comment.

Authors have also taken a one-to-one approach; James Joyce advised Italo Svevo (who initially came to him for English lessons), and Joyce later became mentor to Samuel Beckett. As well as mentoring of emerging writers by more mature ones, there is what we could call co-mentoring, where two writers at a comparable stage of development exchange work: like many novelists, I've done this informally with friends I trust to give an honest and useful opinion. Various formal mentoring schemes exist, I participate in one funded by Scottish Book Trust, working with first-time novelists. The relationship bears some resemblance to that of author and editor; in either case the desired outcomes are artistic progress and publishable product, though we could distinguish between writer-centred or output-centred mentoring, depending on which goal is seen as having greater weight.

While all of these activities involve a learning process, none of them necessarily involves teaching. Writing groups and mentoring partnerships can be a wholly spontaneous, intuitive sharing of ideas, without any element of instruction or imbalance of authority between participants. But there are courses and books that aim to teach creative writing; I am involved in university degree programmes up to PhD. This can be seen as a departure from the purely informal, non-instructional tradition that has lasted for centuries.

As an academic subject in British universities, creative writing is relatively youthful but has developed rapidly. The first MA programme began in 1970 at the University of East Anglia; in 1992 its founder Malcolm Bradbury commented in the *Times Literary Supplement* on the 'massive growth . . . in a subject that not too long ago was regarded as a suspect American import, like the hamburger.'[2] By 2000 there were 40 postgraduate degree courses in British universities, and there are now around a hundred, with creative writing featuring as a component in many undergraduate degrees, such as the joint English Literature and Creative Writing BA on which I teach at Northumbria University.

Being a teacher or graduate of a university creative writing programme has long been a familiar feature of US authors' profiles, but in Britain, until fairly recently, it was almost something to be ashamed of. This has changed. In the *Guardian*'s 'Twelve best new novelists' feature in 2011, John Mullan commented, '[o]f the 57 novels submitted to our panel, almost a third were by graduates of creative writing courses. Invariably, writers who have been on such courses announce the fact in the information printed below the author's photograph on the dustjacket of their first novel. It is as if graduation from such a programme is a further recommendation to the potential reader.'[3] As additional evidence of this new respectability, Mullan cited the appointment of Martin Amis as Professor of Creative Writing at Manchester University (he has since been succeeded by Colm Tóibín). 'A still young subject seemed vindicated', wrote Mullan. Meanwhile writers such as Will Self express the traditional skepticism. 'I'm still not convinced creative writing can be taught', he says. '[U]nless you want to churn out thrillers or misery memoirs, you can't work from a pattern book.'4

Will Self expresses a familiar misunderstanding of what academic creative writing actually is. Literature students study writing through reading, creative writing students study writing through writing. Students already know how to read a book before they enrol for an English degree, and will be able to write a story before embarking on a creative writing course. The aim is not to create a new generation of Booker Prize winners, any more than a physics degree aims to produce the next Einstein.

Part of the problem for our subject is its name. Walk into any British bookshop, ask for "creative writing", and you are unlikely to be led to shelves housing *Madame Bovary* or *War and Peace*. Creative writing, in many minds, suggests activity rather than product, and to the extent that it does apply to product, it can even implicitly diminish it. The idea that Flaubert or Tolstoy were 'creative writers' seems mildly ridiculous: surely they were just 'writers'?

Creativity is a concept born of Romanticism, implying a qualitative and heavily value-laden distinction. As the musician Klesmer puts it in *Daniel Deronda*, 'A creative artist is no more a mere musician than a great states-man is a mere politician.'5 Klesmer represents a European concept of artistic elitism; a virtuoso drilled in a tradition he must conserve and extend. A contrasting tone of democratic individualism was struck by Emerson in his 1837 lecture, 'The American Scholar':

> The soul active sees absolute truth; and utters truth, or creates. In this action, it is genius; not the privilege of here and there a favourite, but the sound estate of every man. In its essence, it is progressive. The book, the college, the school of art, the institution of any kind, stop with some past utterance of genius ... But genius looks forward ... man hopes: genius creates ... There are creative manners, there are creative actions, and creative words; manners, actions, words, that is, indicative

of no custom or authority, but springing spontaneous from the mind's own sense of good and fair . . . One must be an inventor to read well . . . There is then creative reading as well as creative writing.[6]

Along with individualism went commodification: by the 1920s in America, in addition to creative writing courses, there were commercially oriented manuals of composition and marketing, such as *The Business of Writing*.[7] This close association of art and commerce was to be one factor in British resistance to creative writing when it began to establish itself here a half-century later; another was the foregrounding of self-realisation at the expense of traditional scholarship.

At one extreme is the idea that writing cannot be taught or assessed, all value being subjective and relative; at the other is the claim that there exist explainable techniques or principles of good writing. For the subjectivist, the denial of meaningful assessment risks serving as excuse for labour-saving indulgence: if everyone gets 71% then everyone is happy. Or else it may manifest itself in inexpressible gut feeling: the teacher cannot explain why one piece is better than another, it just is. The teacher is then like a guru, or celebrity judge on a talent contest, made authoritative by reputation garnered elsewhere, while for the student there is only a thumbs-up or down.

The instrumentalist, by contrast, has no need of reputation or even experience: rules are all that need be learned. In *A Guide to Fiction Writing*, published in 1936, Kobold Knight urged aspiring authors to produce stories that 'tell themselves', offering prose examples such as:

> The great car took the hairpin bend on two wheels, and the fugitive cast an agonized glance down the winding mountain road. Far below him but drawing ever closer, was the pillar of yellow dust that was the avenger.[8]

Knight's comment on this passage, hackneyed even by the standards of its own time, was, '[i]t is dramatic telling—and it is the only kind of story-telling, speaking broadly, that editors want and will pay for . . . ' Similar advice is offered today, in print or online, couched within the language of advertising and offering answers to questions such as, 'How long should a chapter be?'

Making art is difficult, teaching it should be difficult too. What I teach, and how, are questions to which I never expect to reach a final answer, any more than I expect an ultimate solution to the problem of novel writing. Academic enquiry is the pursuit of knowledge, but knowledge in creative writing is not of the factual, propositional kind that Kobold Knight and his successors would have us believe: the seven or a hundred rules of good writing, as memorable and inviolable as the laws of thermodynamics. Nor is it the historically cumulative knowledge of traditional scholarship in the humanities. Knowledge is a response to questions; artistic knowledge responds to artistic questions.

For the student, specific questions are 'How do I become a writer?' and 'Is my writing any good?' These are questions of process, composition and evaluation. Inevitably this leads to questions of technique and craft, areas that the 'How-to' manuals are apt to approach with familiar rules such as 'write what you know' or 'show don't tell'. Artistic experience teaches us that rules are there to be questioned: who made them up and why? What authority do they have? What examples can be produced in favour or in opposition? This falls recognisably within traditional poetics or stylistics; Wayne Booth's *The Rhetoric Of Fiction*, for example, dealt very ably with 'show don't tell' half a century ago, offering a nuanced counterbalance to what by then had already filtered down from Jamesian criticism into writing-school dogma.[9] More widely, though, we can question the concept of technique. Adorno found it suspect,[10] partly influenced by Lukacs's critique of 'expertise',[11] but specifically in relation to musical composition, which he studied with Alban Berg. The writing school bears some comparison with the musical conservatory, and the latter serves as something of a warning with its ontology of forms (sonata, fugue, and so on). Technique, Adorno argued, becomes external to artistic production, a portable toolbox. This certainly accords with institutional notions of transferable skills, but the artwork that can be seen as an exemplar of a pre-existing standard is one that asserts the validity of that standard and the necessity of its preconditions.

A student once showed me a hand-out she had been given on a creative writing course at an institution other than my own. It mapped out the 'three act structure' for novels, indicating where plot points should occur, graphically represented by the familiar Freytag triangle with its cardinal areas of exposition, climax, denouement. As a way of producing wholly generic storylines for movies (*Star Wars*, *The Lion King*, for example), the morphologies of Aristotle, Gustav Freytag, Joseph Campbell et al. have proved their worth, even if one guesses that such simplicity could be generated well enough by moderately talented minds without need of the astrologically complex theoretical framework used to dignify the end product. With regard to published novels, however, I do not know of any that convincingly demonstrates such a scheme, beyond the fact that its story will have a beginning, middle and end (not necessarily told in that order). Scheme-novels certainly exist (e.g. *Ulysses* or *Life: A User's Manual*), but the significance of those schemes is their uniqueness, not generality. My student's hand-out offered a three-act blueprint without naming a single published example, which from a methodological point of view would appear to be the most elementary flaw imaginable.

Apart from intellectual vacuity, the danger of such instrumentalism is that students find it so appealing. After all, some have entered the academy in hope of being taught how to become rich and famous; others have a less explicit engagement with consumerism but are nevertheless subject to its message that all things are measurable and marketable. Freytag's work on tragic drama[12] or Campbell's narrative pattern of the 'hero's journey'[13] are interesting enough as episodes in the history of ideas, but their claim to value lies in finding patterns in existing works, not in telling us how to produce new ones. If I were studying painting in a nineteenth-century art school then it would be good for me to learn comparative anatomy and discover how the musculature of a horse corresponds to that of a dog or man. But as a painter, I don't want to know that they're all in some sense the same thing, I want to know how to paint dogs that look like dogs rather than horses; in fact, to paint one dog that looks like a unique creature. Knowing there are only seven basic plots in the world, as Christopher Booker argues[14] (or however many there are meant to be) is of equally limited use. The novelist is not interested in narrative as general category (akin to 'mammal'), but in the novel as specific object of construction. Yet despite hearing such caveats, there are always students who will devour any kind of formalism as if it were a magic spell, just as there are those who will reject it as being inherently opposed to creativity. If it works for them, fine.

I'm a professional writer, and at least some of my students want to become professional writers too. My job is to try and help them on their way to doing what I do, even if they want to do it completely differently. Simply by putting it in those terms, I've already taken on a range of assumptions: I actually think of writing as an activity rather than a job description, but conceiving it in economic or institutional terms is at least a start. There is much in any creative writing course that could be said to reflect professional practice. Writers have their work evaluated by editors, booksellers, judging panels and readers, and most importantly they have to try and evaluate it for themselves. But on a university course there is also assessment: tutors have to use their professional expertise (a problematic concept in its own right) to arrive at a mark. The mark has obvious practical importance for students hoping to receive a formal qualification, but how are we to understand the meaning of the mark?

I have already alluded to the subjectivist view that any kind of mark is in some sense fraudulent. Certainly we could say that art is fundamentally concerned with the unquantifiable. Institutionalisation, like professionalisation, is not a necessity of art but an aspect of commodification, and a reality of life. If we are going to have degrees in creative writing then there need to be marks, and practitioners have a duty to make them meaningful.

There is an exercise I like to conduct with my writing students, in which I give them some stories, with no indication of who the authors are, or whether they are published or unpublished, and I ask the students individually to rank the pieces (best to worst, top to bottom, favourite to least favourite: terminology is less important here than process). They discuss their rankings and then possibly revise them; what they are doing is a slightly more formalised version of what judging panels do all the time. What the students learn—in case they didn't already know it—is how difficult, instructive and rewarding such a process can be.

The exercise has some similarity to I. A. Richards' *Practical Criticism*, though Richards used only published texts and asked only for qualitative judgments.[15] My motivation was that I had found that, for myself, the most satisfactory way I could assess a sample of creative pieces was by first rank-ordering them, then assigning marks, where experience over time (and moderation of marks in discussion with co-markers) gradually gave me some sense of appropriate attribution of percentages. Assessment is thus made in comparative rather than absolute terms.

At around the same time that Richards was doing his exercise, in the 1920s, Louis Thurstone made statistical studies of rank ordering in a variety of contexts and came up with his 'Law of Comparative Judgment'. [16] Yet while Thurstone was mathematically rigorous in his studies of judgment, he lacked critical reflection on the nature of what was being judged (considered non-measureable and hence, in his instrumentalised approach, meaningless). And although Richards explicitly concerned himself with critical reflection, it was pursued in a way that produced empirical data of limited value. A similar division can be discerned in Adorno's experience with the Radio Research Project in New York,[17] where he was horrified by a programme reliant on questionnaires and psychometrics, rather than (as he would have wished) analysis of the historical conditions that might have given rise to the categories being measured. The modern field of cognitive humanities concerns itself to some extent with these sorts of issues, though work has tended to be oriented around reading more than writing. Here is a field of creative writing studies where more could certainly be done.

That sort of research question is not what makes any student enrol on a creative writing course. People want to write, and teachers hope to encourage, advise, perhaps inspire. Writers are of all kinds, and they teach in all sorts of ways, a variety that is reassuring and essential. Most of us who teach are primarily writers ourselves, and what we mostly want to do is get on with our own writing. Teaching, under those circumstances, can be simply a way of earning some cash, in which case it is likely to become a chore as demoralising to the student as it is to the unwilling instructor. But it can also bring new ways of thinking about one's own writing, and I would certainly say that it has enabled me to reflect more widely on the philosophy of fiction, as well as on the sort of practical issues that arise in any kind of teaching. In that respect, teaching the novel has the same attraction as writing one: I never know in advance how things will turn out.

NOTES

[1] Stephen King, *On Writing* (London: New English Library, 2001).

[2] Malcolm Bradbury, 'The Bridgeable Gap', *The Times Literary Supplement*, January 17, 1992.

[3] John Mullan, 'Twelve of the best new novelists', *Guardian*, February 25, 2011.

[4] Will Self, in Janet Murray, 'Can You Teach Creative Writing', *Guardian*, May 10, 2011.

[5] George Eliot, *Daniel Deronda* (London: Oxford World's Classics, 1998 [1876]).

[6] R.W. Emerson, 'The American Scholar', in *The Essays of Ralph Waldo Emerson*, eds. A.R. Ferguson and J.F. Carr (New York: Dover, 1987), 852.

[7] R.C. Holliday and A. Van Rensselaer, *The Business of Writing* (New York: George H. Doran Co., 1922).

[8] Kobold Knight, *A Guide to Fiction Writing* (New York: M.S. Mill Co., 1936), 91.

[9] Wayne C. Booth, *The Rhetoric Of Fiction* (Chicago: University of Chicago Press, 1961).

[10] Theodor W. Adorno, A.G. Mitchell and W.V. Blomster, *Philosophy of Modern Music* (London: Continuum, 2004 [1949]).

[11] G. Lukacs, *History and Class Consciousness*, trans. R. Livingstone (Cambridge: MIT Press, 1972 [1923]).

[12] G. Freytag, *Technique of the Drama*, trans. E.J. McEwan (Chicago: Scott, Foresman and Co., 1900).

[13] J. Campbell, *The Hero With A Thousand Faces* (London: Fontana, 1993 [1949]).

[14] Christopher Booker, *The Seven Basic Plots* (London: Continuum, 2005).

[15] I.A. Richards, *Practical Criticism* (London: Routledge, 1991 [1929]).

[16] L.L. Thurstone, 'A law of comparative judgement', *Psychological Review*, 34, (Cambridge: 1927), 273-286.

[17] T.W. Adorno, 'Scientific Experiences of a European Scholar in America', in *The Intellectual Migration*, edss. D. Fleming and Bernard Bailyn, (Harvard University, 1969).

CONTRIBUTORS

Paul Crosthwaite is Lecturer in English Literature at the University of Edinburgh.

Andrew Crumey is a novelist and the former Literary Editor of *Scotland on Sunday*. He is Senior Lecturer in Creative Writing at Northumbria University.

Maureen Freely is a novelist, translator, and journalist. She is Professor of Creative Writing at Warwick University.

Jennifer Hodgson is a PhD researcher at Durham University and UK Editor at Dalkey Archive Press.

Stewart Home is a writer and artist.

Jamie George is an artist working in London.

Carole Jones is Lecturer in English Literature at the University of Edinburgh.

China Miéville is a novelist and three-time winner of the Arthur C. Clarke Award.

Victor Sage is Emeritus Professor of Literature at the University of East Anglia.

Berthold Schoene is Professor of English and Director of the Institute for Humanities and Social Science Research at Manchester Metropolitan University.

Katy Shaw is Senior Lecturer and Head of Subject in Contemporary Literature at the University of Brighton.

Patricia Waugh is Professor of English Studies at Durham University.

BOOK REVIEWS

Clarice Lispector. *Near to the Wild Heart*. Trans. Alison Entrekin. Intro. Benjamin Moser. New Directions, 2012. 196 pp. Paper: $15.95.

Brazilian writer Clarice Lispector's first novel, *Near to the Wild Heart*, was published to much acclaim in 1943 when she was only twenty-three years old. An intensely introspective and philosophical novel, it has much to offer contemporary readers interested in the big questions (*who am I, why am I here, what will be the shape of my life?*), framed in formally innovative ways. It is in many ways a coming-of-age novel, tracing the development of a young, intelligent, and disaffected woman from her earliest childhood memories to the dissolution of her marriage. Often employing a stream of consciousness discourse, *Near to the Wild Heart* has been described as Joycean, (the title is a quote from Joyce), but this designation has to do more with form than content. Joana, the young protagonist, while possessing the writer's powers of observation and sense of ethical acuity, is here not concerned with art making or with culture per se. Instead, her preoccupations are existential, concerned fundamentally with her place in society and her relationships with others as social facts, as per Camus in *The Stranger* and Sartre in *The Wall*. These questions are explored in a subjective manner, framed from her point of view and intertwined with a vigorous and pervasive pantheism that could owe much to Lispector's interest in seventeenth-century philosopher Spinoza. Given the novel's thematic ambitions, some may find the book slow going, but patient readers will be rewarded, as around two thirds of the way through, the ideals and choices of the protagonist are put to the test. Joana finds that her husband Octavio has been having an affair with another woman, Lidia, and that she is now with child. Joana goes to see Lidia, and their confrontation is riveting in its emotional precision and thematic resonance; it's a highly memorable and surprising scene, one that will stay with an appreciative, adventuresome reader for quite a while. [Gary Lain]

José Saramago. *The Lives of Things*. Trans. Giovanni Pontiero. Verso, 2012. 145 pp. Cloth: $23.95

For the fan of José Saramago's work, *The Lives of Things,* a collection of the writer's early experiments with the short story, is like stepping into a candy store with all the young novelist's growing powers on display. Originally published in 1978, four years before Saramago hit the world stage with *Baltasar and Blimunda,* we can already find the author's distinctive ability to balance incisive statements with imaginative digressions. While stories like "The Centaur" or "Revenge" could be described as Kafkaesque, other stories, such as "The Chair" and "Embargo," not only offer early signs of Saramago's trademark political allegories but also give us a glimpse into the satiric voice we've come to associate with a man who has been hailed as one of the world's great novelists: "If they were to say the same thing, if they were to group together through affinity of structure and origin, then life would be much simpler, by means of successive reduction, down to onomatopoeia which is not simple either." Although Saramago's idiosyncratic style is clearly on display in these early stories, he has not quite perfected the power of the comma evident in his later work. Interestingly, the suppressed first person plural narrator we've come to associate with the author is only on display in about half of these stories. After reading this collection, the Saramago aficionado feels he or she has been immersed in a writer beginning to explore the potential of his formal innovations, but already fully at home in his thematic concerns. Every story, as can be said of so many of Saramago's novels, concerns itself at some level with death. In Saramago's universe, death is not necessarily an end but often marks the potential for transformation, as in these final lines of "The Centaur": "Then he looked at his body. It was bleeding. Half a man. A man. And he saw the gods approaching. It was time to die." [Peter Grandbois]

Ivan Vladislavić. *A Labour of Moles*. Sylph Editions, 2012. 46 pp. Paper: $19.00.

A *labour* of moles is the collective term for the animal. And while in a figurative sense the unnamed narrator of this short tale may be said to burrow into the mystery with which he is presented at the start, tunneling his way toward self-realization, actual moles do figure in the narrative as clever creatures who represent more than their first appearance may suggest. Understanding their purpose ultimately helps to prompt the gradual awakening of the narrator to his unique situation, for from the outset, bewildered by his novel circumstances, he is driven to learn precisely where he is. Seemingly dropped from the sky, he has only the dimmest notion of where he was beforehand as he scrambles about a world in which time seems absent, place indeterminate, and the things he confronts an oddly assorted lot, only one of which, a statue, seems able to communicate with him. This cautious if friendly figure, a marble sculpture of a Murderer, implies that one ordering principle of this peculiar environment is the alphabet, as he proceeds to rattle off a slew of objects and concepts surrounding the pair which begin with the letter M. Despite his appearance, wearing a toga and clutching a bloody knife, an indispensable part of his nature, the Murderer means to be helpful and possesses a mocking sense of humor. Through his influence the narrator, who can move around, unlike the statue, sets off to find the land of P, and later, other new worlds of words which, once he has begun to view himself as the Murderer suggests, promise a reward of untold possibilities awaiting him. This delightfully playful tale is interspersed with a series of intricate line drawings from *The English Duden* (1937), which offer their own distinct counterpoint and implicit commentary throughout the volume. [Michael Pinker]

Gabriele D'Annunzio. *Notturno*. Trans. Stephen Sartarelli. Preface Virginia Jewiss. Yale Univ. Press, 2011. 329 pp. Cloth: $28.00.

Flamboyant and charismatic, Gabriele D'Annunzio enjoyed immense popularity during his lifetime as a novelist, poet, and playwright, at least in part thanks to his extraliterary celebrity—from his military exploits to his *affaires de coeur*. His fame was accelerated by the appearance of *Notturno* (1921), a memoir devoted to "the peerless music of godly war" and to anguished, prideful self-assessment that bleeds frequently into self-glorification. With both eyes bandaged following an airplane crash during a wartime mission over Trieste, D'Annunzio wrote *Notturno* on several thousand thin strips of paper, a line or two on each, "the way the Sibyls used to write their brief auguries. . . ." The result is straightforward recollection mixed with hallucinated prose poem, a militant Futurism articulated in what translator Stephen Sartarelli describes as an "often antiquated style." The book finds room to deify his mother, anatomize his painful convalescence, recall his boyhood and remembered landscapes, eulogize his daughter, and conjure dripping faucets, walks in the Venice fog, violets and violins. Primarily, however, *Notturno* is a patriotic paean to the comradeship of soldiers, offering profound glimpses into the mentality of men wholly committed to a cause they are willing—indeed, eager—to die for. The reader, however, must have a high tolerance for romantic gush and a willingness to see past what we also know about D'Annunzio: that he was a fascist and warmonger. Although claiming his "insatiable" loves know no guilt, he asks at one point, "What sin am I expiating?" Well, more than 650,000 Italian soldiers died in WWI, which I would have thought a sufficient answer. Nevertheless, *Notturno* constituted a singular accomplishment in the unfolding of Italian modernism (not least for proving a popular as well as aesthetic success), and it remains a challenging, provocative text for readers who must reconcile a charming self-portrait and an attractive narrative voice with sometimes appalling ideals. [Brooke Horvath]

Alan Singer. *The Inquisitor's Tongue*. FC2, 2012. 259 pp. Paper: $16.95.

The Inquisitor's Tongue is a double narrative set during the Spanish Inquisition. The first is the confession of Osvaldo, a *converso* or convert from Judaism, whose opening statement ("I am not myself") initiates an extended meditation on identity. As a Christian by adoption, he repeatedly refers to himself as an imposter acting out roles over which falls the shadow of torture and execution. The second narrative is delivered by an official of the Inquisition who is reading this confession to an individual under investigation and constantly challenging the latter's interpretations of events. Singer's alternation of narrative strands moves the reader in and out of Osvaldo's story and also establishes a general condition of doubleness in the novel as a whole. Osvaldo has a brother who is an ordained priest and who functions as an alternative self. The very title of the novel puns on double meanings, suggesting at once the organ of speech and that of taste. Osvaldo rises in status within his patron cardinal's establishment by becoming an expert wine taster, a skill where his brief verdicts replace any more elaborate utterances since speech itself becomes life threatening in the context of the Inquisition. The novel makes impressive use of the elaborate symbols and rituals of Spanish Catholicism, depicting them as thinly disguised forms of sensuality and superstition. As *The Inquisitor's Tongue* moves towards its conclusion, the two narratives gradually converge, characters in one blurring into figures from the other. The action is grimly framed by graphic executions—quartering, burning, and poisoning among others—all carried out the name of an institutionalized faith in truth that the novel repeatedly questions. Osvaldo's story begins with him finding a dismembered leg left at his door. Is this a warning of his ultimate fate? The fact that it reminds him of a question mark hints at the ambiguity of signs that characterizes the novel as a whole. Although Singer has clearly researched the historical dimension to the action, the novel demonstrates a postmodern awareness of the duplicity of language itself. [David Seed]

Iosi Havilio. *Open Door*. Trans. Beth Fowler. Afterword Oscar Guardiola-Rivera. And Other Stories, 2011. Paper: 218 pp. Paper: £10.00.

Spoiler alert: There's no spoiling *Open Door*, Iosi Havilio's enigmatic first novel. One could say it centers on the disappearance of the protagonist's lover Aída. Or one could say it's about the protagonist's vacillation post-disappearance between Jaime, a hapless country bachelor, and the seductive innocent Eloísa. Or one could say it's an investigation of the titular psychiatric facility where Jaime works, which treats patients using the "open door method" which holds that "lunatics are made furious by precisely the coercion that is exercised on their liberty, the liberty to come and go, to move about." The narrative proceeds through bifurcation as the protagonist chooses one path, then another, or she chooses neither; not surprisingly, Oscar Guardiola-Rivera's provocative afterword alludes to Borges and David Lynch in situating Havilio's work. In Beth Fowler's muscular, suggestive translation, character and atmosphere are constantly shifting between extremes of stasis and violence, apathy and longing: "On the way to the stable, Jaime tells me that the horse is called Jaime, like him." This sentence represents in microcosm the texture of *Open Door*, which by turns renders coincidence with the heft of fate, and fate as absurd happenstance. Guardiola-Rivera offers an intriguing key to this puzzle of a novel. Whether or not they agree, readers will have a hard time leaving *Open Door*. [Pedro Ponce]

Brian Evenson. *Windeye*. Coffee House Press, 2012. 188 pp. Paper: $16.00.

Brian Evenson's latest collection of stories recalls the psychological ambiguities of Poe, the dark humor of Kafka, and the radically uncertain entropic worlds of Samuel Beckett's later fictions. The result is a blend of horror, fantasy, and sci-fi in a particularly metafictional, "literary" mode, and it is this peculiarly metafictional sensibility that makes the stories more than just creepy tales in the tradition of *The Twilight Zone* or *Tales from the Crypt*. To be sure, in *Windeye* psychopathic murderers triumph, characters are locked in labyrinthine hells of their minds and environments, and body parts have wills of their own. Yet, often tinged with as much humor as horror (the wonderful speculative story about AC/DC's Bon Scott joining a Mormon choir before his "suspicious" death), Evenson's real contribution to this literary oleo is in returning it to the act of storytelling and narrative itself, just as Poe does in *The Narrative of Arthur Gordon Pym*. For the eternal problem in Evenson's stories is: how can a story be told by a dead, possibly dead, or soon to be dead narrator? Such a dilemma, however, reminds us that all narrative is based on our faulty knowledge of a "real" world. What may, then, seem to be abrupt endings, but which simply confirm the ambiguity or continuation of a bizarre set of circumstances, only underscores Evenson's project. The effect of the endings is cumulative. As each story moves implausibly to its (im)possible end, the sense is that language cannot contain all the slippages of sense and sensibility. These endings are not really endings at all, and the only true dismal ending is when we reach the end of *Windeye*. But, of course, it is at this end that Evenson is already ahead of us, writing new ones. [Ralph Clare]

Eugene Lim. *The Strangers*. Black Square Editions, 2013. 168 pp. Paper: $15.00.

At one point in Eugene Lim's portmanteau novel, a character describes an avant-garde filmmaker's late work as "mysterious, self-erasing, self-denying narratives." Lim's elegant expression is a key to his densely populated and multifaceted fiction, where stories and characters madly proliferate. Yet, despite the narrative fission, Lim's complex, "unstable" characters will sometimes come to resemble one another. On occasion they will fuse—if only momentarily, for estrangement is one of Lim's themes. What seems at first to be an organism shedding fiction after fiction in pursuit of its own perpetuation will be seen within the novel's final sections as an intelligence animated by "the idea that life is just one thing trying out different forms" and that, regardless of their manifold content, "stories [are] linked, [are] locked, [are] constructed together." To have confirmed the fundamental unity of our contingent existence from a welter of fragments and anecdotes is part of Lim's achievement. To place the storytelling act at the center of a novel is a risky strategy: the stories must fascinate. Lim's stories do (except those few that he deliberately effaces as if to give a graphic representation of self-erasure). They have the exoticism, emotional authenticity, and intellectual depth to ensure that the reader will be enthralled. Lim's knowledge of economic theory, political science, art history and practice, the minutiae and mechanisms of businesses large and small is sweeping. His verbal constructions exhibit lyrical and playful strains, indignation and sensuality, and a genuinely hip, idiomatic flair. Lim's ambition to relate "grand narratives"—to tessellate them within a mysterious, comprehensive verbal construction and, in so doing, to recreate in his fictional universe the entire world and its archetypical figures—makes his novel an uncommon artifact. *The Strangers* in its complex self-referential, multi-layered structure, anecdotal mass, and restless inventiveness demands and rewards more than one reading. [Norman Lock]

Aimee Parkison. *The Innocent Party: Stories*. BOA Editons, 2012. 174 pp. Paper: $14.00.

"Falling after rain, the wet [sparrow] eggs later break in the gutter, a stream of fractured limbs on the concrete ground of the theater alley." It is a disconcerting image, at once immediate and surreal, razor clear yet inaccessible as if glimpsed in a dream. Like so many of her generation, raised entirely within the reach of visual technology, Aimee Parkison, whose stories have garnered both critical praise and prestigious awards, maintains a voyeur's densely layered dynamic with the world. In these newest stories, it is easy to get seduced as much by the sonic texture of her accomplished prose as by its startling cinematic imagery. But make no mistake—Parkison is a storyteller, conjuring characters who harbor festering secrets, lurid urgencies, and violent compulsions. Like Joyce Carol Oates, Parkison deftly works the caricatures of Southern Gothicism into terrifying clarity. In "Dummy," a woman, devastated by guilt after her lesbian lover leaps to her death, summons her ghost—theirs a complex Jamesian relationship that turns stunningly into a dark celebration of the liberating empowerment of suicide itself. Again and again Parkison plays with expectations, pivoting her characters into provocative dimensions. In the opening story, for instance, "Paints and Papers," an aging painter is attacked, his skull cracked open. Yet the damage realigns his vision—he now sees vividly into supernatural dimensions of vibrant color and intoxicating, erotic play. The collection's centerpiece narrative, "Allison's Idea," is a Carver-meets-Poe tale of spoiled college girls who, searching for a pet, impulsively buy two children through the black market; this turns into a harrowing (and genuinely frightening) tale of cruelty that becomes a dark allegory for contemporary parenting. Parkison's tales are bedtime stories, best read just before surrendering to the heavy drag of sleep, the threshold landscape most appropriate to Parkison's most arresting sensibility. [Joseph Dewey]

Ryunosuke Akutagawa. *A Fool's Life*. Trans. Anthony Barnett and Toraiwa Naoko. Allardyce, Barnett, Publishers, 2007. 64 pp. Paper: $24.00.

The fifty-one third-person scraps and fragments that constitute Ryunosuke Akutagawa's *A Fool's Life* chronicle the existence of a suicidal aesthete in fin-de-siècle Japan. The aesthete in question is, of course, Akutagawa himself, best known now, perhaps, as the author of "Rashōmon," the story upon which Akira Kurosawa based his film of the same name. The form, if not the content, of the short pieces here collected—none are as long as a page—will call to mind the work of currently (and justly) popular miniaturists such as Lydia

Davis, though Akutagawa is more portentous than Davis allows herself to be. Given that his notes about a suicide were penned by a suicide during his final days, this is not, perhaps, surprising, but Akutagawa, with his laconic prose and his eschewal of emotional slop, reminds us that even notes written in profound pain, pain that will not ultimately be vanquished, need not degenerate into maudlin and "redemptive" pain-porn. Akutagawa, in both his life and his work, always placed art first, so it's no surprise that *A Fool's Life* is artful rather than therapeutic. Nietzsche, Verlaine, Dostoevsky, Baudelaire—names to conjure with in early twentieth-century Japan—were among his idols, and Akutagawa invokes these guides in the opening vignette. The protagonist stands on a bookstore ladder "reading the letters on the spines of the books." He glances down at the salesclerks and customers. "They appeared," Akutakagawa writes, "strangely small. Indeed, quite wretched." The power of art—the books he studies perched on the ladder—mixed with the alienation and madness art can bring is the miasma that hangs over this fragmented life of a fool, a miasma that, for Akutagawa, only thickened. Art retained its power; madness and death arrived. This artful scattering remains. [David Cozy]

Franz Werfel. *Pale Blue Ink in a Lady's Hand*. Trans. James Reidel. David R. Godine, 2012. 144 pp. Paper: $17.95.

For a writer looking to reveal the darker forces concealed beneath a refined and beautiful surface, Vienna in the years before the Anschluss presents an ideal setting. In his novella *Pale Blue Ink in a Lady's Hand*, Franz Werfel masterfully draws out the contrast between the former imperial capital's urbane sophistication and the moral emptiness at its core. Werfel's accomplishment is all the more impressive in the degree to which the book itself embodies this contrast, appearing to be a domestic drama about a long-ago fling of a lion of high society before the far more sinister reality behind the story's events finally comes to light. The writing is powerfully concise throughout. There are no descriptions of characters, settings or even the weather that don't have a compelling symbolic role. Werfel recounts the rise of Leonidas Tachezy into wealth and position against a backdrop of mundane external events that take place over the course of a single day—Leonidas sees a letter with familiar handwriting, agonizes over and eventually reads it, concludes that his old affair resulted in a son, goes to work, takes a walk, attempts to deal with the consequences of his fling. Yet what makes the novella so powerful is the inquisition the self-satisfied bureaucrat is subjected to as the false veneer of his life is stripped away layer by layer. What remains is the cruel fate suffered by the Jews that seem to have played such vital parts in his storybook life. Another writer might have shown scenes of Nazi brutality to emphasize the barbarity that actually sets this day of harsh realization in motion. Instead, Werfel makes do with a single mention of the word torture, letting its offhand, incongruous entry into the sedate surroundings of a Vienna hotel lobby strike with explosive force. [Michael Stein]

William O'Rourke. *Confessions of a Guilty Freelancer*. Indiana Univ. Press, 2012. 355 pp. Paper: $29.00.

William O'Rourke is that rare writer to have published a report on a contemporary event and to live to see it become an enduring classic. The University of Notre Dame Press has just this year (2012) republished his *The Harrisburg 7 and the New Catholic Left*. The basic reason for its endurance? The clarity of prose reflecting O'Rourke's now life-long acknowledgment of his early mentor Edward Dahlberg. The same could be said of his modest first novel, *The Meekness of Isaac*, which is also overdue for reissue. *Confessions of a Guilty Freelancer* collects book reviews, articles, and occasional journalism, complimenting an earlier collection, *Signs of the Literary Times: Essays, Reviews, Profiles 1970–1992*. Here, in a review of Raymond Carver stories, O'Rourke has set down one of the saddest and most disturbing lines I have read in many years. He is writing about some reviews he was working on for his local paper: "Since the book reviews in the *South Bend Tribune* are not indexed anywhere, our daily town paper being the proverbial fish wrap, it is not likely any present reader has read what I had to say." O'Rourke's descriptions of the writing life have the ring of absolute truth. I found myself underlining, turning down corners: "[A]s any writer of books knows, there are three things one hopes for: to be published, to be reviewed and to turn up in bookstores. What one learns is one of those must happen (publication), but it is even more difficult to capture all three." Still, O'Rourke's explicitly personal essays are the most moving; the simple piece "Dear Dad" opens with the sure touch that belongs only to him: "I am struck by the fact that this may be the first time in my fifty-two years of life I have written Dear Dad, addressed only you in a letter, not both you and mom, father and mother, parents." This book is exacting description of a writer's life at the turn of centuries. Beware. [Thomas McGonigle]

Susan Sontag. *As Consciousness is Harnessed to Flesh: Journals & Notebooks, 1964-1980*. Farrar, Straus & Giroux, 2012. 544 pp. Cloth: $30.00.

In the mid-1960s—newly returned from abroad, freshly divorced, an inaugural contributor to the *New York Review of Books*, and still in her thirties—Susan Sontag was chic and brilliantly supercilious: a reluctant American of acquired European taste and sensibility, powerfully charming at will. The second volume of her *Journals & Notebooks*—edited by her son, David Rieff—spans about a decade and a half of Sontag's fame, travel, intense work, illness, and recovery (1964–1980). As they begin, the success of her "Notes on 'Camp'" and the other seminal essays collected in *Against Interpretation* have freed Sontag to enjoy her renown as cultural critic, both at home in New York and on working sojourns in France, Morocco, Sweden, etc. But the reflections on style, the marginalia on art, the lists of novels and films, all generously accumulated here, eclipse autobiography, amounting instead to "waste books" affectionately modeled on those of Georg Christoph Lichtenberg. The great European modernists, the exiles—whose seriousness she first tasted as a child in California, at tea with Thomas Mann—are present throughout, giving the impression of a universal project to which Sontag's favored contemporary writers all managed somehow to contribute. In spite of this private bounty, the wallpaper of Sontag's inner life is, at times, painfully impersonal. Though she possessed, or was possessed by, the "ancient compulsion to populate the world with 'culture' and information," the avid cultivation of her taste was borne of a dire need "to fill myself up." As Rieff notes, unhappiness haunted these years. There were frustrated novels, abandoned screenplays, and three years of cancer treatment yielding no journal notes, though the episode brought about the monumental *Illness as Metaphor*. By 1980, when Sontag had both become a fellow at NYU's Institute for the Humanities and fully dropped her communist sympathies under the influence of Joseph Brodsky, the notebooks show as little biographical punctuation as ever. To read the personal papers of a writer is to glance into the psychic effects of unseen—that is, compositional—choices, but also to encounter, in a more diffuse way, the "spiritual project" that guided the pen. In Sontag's case, her self-directed injunction—to actively contain and transmit what was worth knowing—is punctuation enough. [Amy Kerner]

Stephen J. Burn. *David Foster Wallace's* Infinite Jest: *A Reader's Guide* (Second Edition). Continuum, 2012. 144 pp. Paper: $19.95; Samuel Cohen and Lee Konstantinou, eds. *The Legacy of David Foster Wallace*. Univ. of Iowa Press, 2012. 296 pp. Paper: $19.95.

"Communication, connection, difficult, human, irony, mediate, personal, sadness, suffering . . . these are the words overwhelmingly deployed" throughout *The Legacy of David Foster Wallace*, presented (in alphabetical order) by the editors of this collection of critical essays and remembrances by both Wallace scholars and the author's contemporaries—including Don DeLillo, Dave Eggers, Jonathan Franzen, and Nick Moody. These "key words," which also appear repeatedly in Stephen J. Burn's *David Foster Wallace's* Infinite Jest: *A Reader's Guide* (Second Edition), underlie both volumes' discussion of Wallace's continuing influence on contemporary fiction and of his projected influence on its future, prospectively dubbed "Postironic Belief" by Lee Konstantinou in his essay "No Bull."

It's no mistake that the first chapter of Burn's revised and expanded second edition bears the similar title "David Foster Wallace's Legacy." In the aftermath of a tragedy—the premature loss of one of contemporary fiction's most gifted writers—this updated edition reexamines the sadness and suffering seemingly ever-present in Wallace's work, tempered by (and sometimes hidden beneath) Wallace's sharp wit, compassionate sensibility, and playful rapport with the reader. While neither volume dwells upon the sadness and suffering felt by Wallace's scholars, critics, and loyal—if not downright reverential—fans, these key words are incorporated into the larger discussion of the author's unique ability to connect with and inspire empathy in the reader. Set in opposition to the more narcissistic *sym*pathy in which "one projects one's own feelings onto another…taking over, rather than making space for, the other person's feelings"—*em*pathy (in "Infinite Summer," Kathleen Fitzpatrick's essay on communal reading groups of *IJ*) enacts a "kind of ethical engagement with a text—a mode of engagement that encourages a critical awareness of the unresolvable alterity of self and Other, an understanding, rather than an erasure, of difference."

A clear indication of Wallace's influence lies in the accessible prose of his scholars. This inviting tone is clearly evident, both in Burn's newly-added career-overview of DFW's poetics and his eye-opening analysis/explanation of *Infinite Jest* (including a chronological de-fragmentation of the novel's main events), as well as in the essays contained in *Legacy*. The editors of the latter volume in particular employ elements of Wallace's offbeat humor, his fluid tonal shifts between high and low registers, and his digressive approach to linear prose—affirming (in an endnote to the introduction): "If Wallace teaches us anything it's that you should be the sort of person who not only obligingly follows footnotes and endnotes but finds great value in doing so." Approachable to all levels Wallace readers, both volumes inform previous readings and will compel any reader, critic or fanatic, to delve deeper into the work of David Foster Wallace. [David Ball]

Books Received

Adán, Martín. *The Cardboard House*. Trans. Katherine Silver. New Directions, 2012. Paper: $13.95. (F)

Bertino, Marie-Helene. *Safe as Houses*. University of Iowa Press, 2012. Paper: $16.00. (F)

Binder, L. Annette. *Rise*. Sarabande, 2012. Paper: $15.95. (F)

Blas de Roblès, Jean-Marie. *Where Tigers Are At Home*. Trans. Mike Mitchell. Other Press, 2013. Cloth: $32.50. (F)

Boianjiu, Shani. *The People of Forever Are Not Afraid*. Hogarth, 2012. Cloth: $24.00. (F)

Brandon, John. *A Million Heavens*. McSweeney's, 2012. Cloth: $24.00. (F)

Buckeye, Robert. *Fade*. Amandla, 2012. Paper: $15.00. (F)

Calasso, Roberto. *La Folie Baudelaire*. Trans. Alastair McEwen. Farrar, Straus and Giroux, 2012. Cloth: $35.00. (NF)

Carthage, David. *The Jericho River*. Winifred, 2012. Paper: $12.50. (F)

Ciocia, Stefania. *Vietnam and Beyond: Tim O'Brien and the Power of Storytelling*. Liverpool University Press, 2012. Cloth: £65.00. (NF)

Corasanti, Michelle Cohen. *The Almond Tree*. Garnet, 2012. Paper: $14.95. (F)

Crandell, Doug. *They're Calling You Home*. Switchgrass, 2012. Paper: $16.00. (F)

Defoe, Gideon. *The Pirates! In an Adventure with the Romantics*. Vintage, 2012. Paper: $14.95. (F)

Dung, Kai-cheung. *Atlas: The Archaeology of an Imaginary City*. Trans. Kai-cheung Dung , Anders Hansson, and Bonnie S. McDougall. Columbia University Press, 2012. Cloth: $ 24.50. (F)

Dungy, Camille T. and Daniel Hahn, eds. *Passageways*. Two Lines, 2012. Paper: $14.95. (F)

Durham, Carolyn A. *Understanding Diane Johnson*. The University of South Carolina Press, 2012. Cloth: $39.95. (NF)

Forrest, Tara, ed. *Alexander Kluge: Raw Materials for the Imagination.* Amsterdam University Press, 2012. Paper: $39.95. (NF)

Gerdes, Eckhard. *The Sylvia Plath Cookbook: A Satire.* Sugar Glider, 2012. Paper: No Price Listed. (F)

Gerdes, Eckhard. *Three Psychedelic Novellas.* Enigmatic Ink, 2012. Paper: $9.99. (F)

Gillespie, William. *Keyhole Factory.* Soft Skull, 2012. Paper: $16.95. (F)

Hanshe, Rainer J. *The Abdication.* Contra Mundum, 2012. Paper: $20.00. (F)

Harvey, Phil. *Show Time.* Lost Coast, 2012. Paper: $15.95. (F)

Hawkins, Bobbie Louise. Ed. Barbara Henning. *Selected Prose of Bobbie Louise Hawkins.* BlazeVOX, 2012. Paper: $18.00. (F)

Hayles, N. Katherine. *How We Think: Digital Media and Contemporary Technogenesis.* The University of Chicago Press, 2012. Paper: $25.00. (NF)

Henderson, Gretchen E. *The House Enters the Street.* Starcherone Books, 2012. Paper: $16.00. (F)

Jergović, Miljenko. *Mama Leone.* Trans. David Williams. Archipelago, 2012. Paper: $16.00 (F)

Johnson, Kent. *A Question Mark Above the Sun.* Starcherone Books, 2012. Paper: $16.00. (F)

Karasu, Bilge. *A Long Day's Evening.* Trans. Aron Aji and Fred Stark. City Lights, 2012. Paper: $13.95. (F)

Kelk, Lindsey. *I Heart Paris.* William Morrow, 2012. Paper: $14.99. (F)

Kendall, Stuart. *Gilgamesh.* Contra Mundum, 2012. Paper: $18.00. (F)

Lam, Vincent. *The Headmaster's Wager.* Hogarth, 2012. Cloth: $25.00. (F)

Leving, Yuri, ed. *Anatomy of a Short Story: Nabokov's Puzzles, Codes, "Signs and Symbols."* Continuum, 2012. Paper: $34.95. (NF)

Lock, Norman. *Escher's Journal.* Ravenna Press, 2012. Paper: $11.95. (F)

Luca, Ghérasim. *Self-Shadowing Prey.* Trans. Mary Ann Caws. Contra Mundum, 2012. Paper: $18.00. (P)

McCleary, Kathleen. *A Simple Thing.* William Morrow, 2012. Paper: $14.99. (F)

Meads, Kat. *For You, Madam Lenin.* Livingston, 2012. Cloth: $30.00. (F)

Meguid, Ibrahim Abdel. *The House of Jasmine.* Trans. Noha Radwan.

Interlink, 2012. Paper: $15.00. (F)

Michon, Pierre. *The Eleven*. Trans. Elizabeth Deshays and Jody Gladding. Archipelago, 2013. Paper: $18.00. (F)

Moreno, Juan Velasco. *La Massacre de los Soñadores/Massacre of the Dreamers*. Trans. Brendan P. Riley. Editorial Polibea, 2010. Paper: No Price Listed. (P)

Muldoon, Paul. *The Word on the Street: Rock Lyrics*. Farrar, Straus and Giroux, 2013. Cloth: $23.00. (P)

Murphet, Julian, and Mark Steven, eds. *Styles of Extinction*: *Cormac McCarthy's* The Road. Continuum, 2012. Paper: $29.95. (NF)

Palumbo-Liu, David. *The Deliverance of Others: Reading Literature in a Global Age*. Duke University Press, 2012. Paper: $23.95. (NF)

Peacock, James. *Jonathan Lethem*. Manchester University Press, 2012. Cloth: $95.00. (NF)

Riddlebarger, Bram. *Earplugs*. Livingston, 2012. Paper: $17.95. (F)

Savage, Sam. *The Way of the Dog*. Coffee House, 2013. Paper: $14.95. (F)

Seidel, Frederick. *Nice Weather*. Farrar, Straus and Giroux, 2012. Cloth: $24.00. (P)

Simpson, Chad. *Tell Everyone I Said Hi*. University of Iowa Press, 2012. Paper: $16.00. (F)

Skemer, Arnold. *I*. Phrygian Press, 2011. Paper: $10.00. (F)

Sreenivasan, Jyotsna. *And Laughter Fell from the Sky*. William Morrow, 2012. Paper: $14.99. (F)

Steiner, Uwe. *Walter Benjamin: An Introduction to His Work and Thought*. Trans. Michael Winkler. The University of Chicago Press, 2012. Paper: $20.00. (NF)

Tillet, Salamishah. *Sites of Slavery: Citizenship and Racial Democracy in the Post-Civil Rights Imagination*. Duke University Press, 2012. Paper: $23.95. (NF)

Tullius, Mark. *Brightside*. Vincere, 2012. Paper: $13.99. (F)

Valle-Inclán, Ramón del. *Tyrant Banderas*. Trans. Peter Bush. New York Review Books, 2012. Paper: $14.95. (F)

Viegner, Matias. *2500 Random Things About Me Too.* Les Figues Press, 2012. Paper: $15.00. (F)

Vivian, Robert. *The Mover of Bones.* Bison Books, 2012. Paper: $14.95. (F)

Youssef, Saadi. *Nostalgia, My Enemy.* Trans. Sinan Antoon and Peter Money. Graywolf, 2012. Paper: $15.00. (P)

Zell, Michael Allen. *Errata.* Lavender Ink, 2012. Paper: $15.00. (F)

Annual Index for Volume XXXII

Contributors

Ballowe, James. "Letter to Bob Coover on Revisiting *The Origin of the Brunists* and Related Letters, 1961–1967," 1: 186–189.

Barth, John. "The Imp of the Perverse," 1: 17–18.

Bell, Elisabeth Ly. "Robert Coover and the Neverending Story of Pinocchio," 1: 32–46.

Bernheimer, Kate. "1. Robert Coover, Miracle Worker," 1: 47–49.

—. "2. Robert Coover, the Author," 1: 87.

—. "3. Robert Coover, Master of Fairy Stories," 1: 258.

Borchardt, Georges. "I First Met Robert Coover..." 1: 207–209.

Caponegro, Mary. "Spanking the Form," 1: 91–96.

Cayley, John. "Period Bob," 1: 156–160.

Chénetier, Marc. "Charlie's Death," 1: 71–77.

Corin, Lucy. "Songs for Sirens, Ditties for Titties," 1: 23–26.

Crosthwaite, Paul. "'Soon the Economic System Will Crumble': Financial Crisis and Contemporary British Avant-Garde Writing," 3: 38–48.

Crumey, Andrew. "Teaching Creative Writing," 3: 114–123.

Ducornet, Rikki. "Fragments of Phallic WivesE," 1: 270.

Epstein, Paul A. "Variations and Approximations," 1: 138–150.

Evenson, Brian. "Robert Coover Tribute," 1: 151–155.

Everett, Percival. "Between Here and There (For Robert Coover)," 1: 216–218.

Field, Thalia. "Coover's Punch," 1: 27–31.

Freely, Maureen. "The Strange Case of the Reader and the Invisible Hand," 3: 30–37.

Gass, William. "Bob, Bill, and Belief," 1: 78–86.

Green, Geoffrey. "Robert Coover: A Vertical Tasting," 1: 50–53.

Hœpffner, Bernard. "Translating Coover, and Bob's My Uncle... (Thoughts of a Grateful Translator)," 1: 106–108.

Hodgson, Jennifer. "An Interview with Jim Crace," 3: 49–61.

—. "Introduction," 3:9–29.

Home, Stewart. "Humanity Will Not Be Happy until the Last Man Booker Prize Winner Is Hung by the Guts of the Final Recipient of the Nobel Prize for Literature!" 3: 72–78.

Hume, Kathryn. "Facing Life's Limits in Robert Coover's Recent Fiction," 1: 56–70.

Ickstadt, Heinz. "Robert in the House of Tales," 1: 238–257.

Jackson, Shelley. "1005 Nights," 1: 97–105.

Jones, Carole. "Post-Meta-Modern-Realism–the Novel in Scotland," 3: 79–86.

Jonke, Gert. "Individual and Metamorphosis," 2: 29–70.

Joyce, Michael. "Introducing Robert Coover (A Mixtape by Request)," 1: 161–177.

Kling, Vincent. "Inventing the Self: Gert Jonke's Fragments of a Great Confession," 2: 11–28.

Masoliver, Juan Antonio. "A Bob Coover, Hechicero de la Palabra, *Grand Cru* de la Amistad (For Bob Coover, Sorcerer of Words, and *Grand Cru* Friend)," 1: 182–185.

Miéville, China. "5 to Read," 3: 98–104.

Moody, Rick. "Syllabus (For Robert Coover)," 1: 259–269.

Morrow, Bradford. "Robert Coover," 1: 54–55.

Olson, Toby. "Out of the Corner of the Eye: A Look at Robert Coover's *Noir*," 1: 109–113.

Parsipur, Shahrnush. "The First Time I Heard the Name Robert Coover..." 1: 88–90.

Porter, Joe Ashby. "For Bob," 1: 19–22.

Quinn, Paul. "The Missing, the No-Longer, and the Not-Yet: Reading Robert Coover's "Apostrophe Trilogy"," 1: 114–137.

Raffel, Dawn. "The Baby," 1: 235–237.

Sage, Victor. "The Ambivalence of Laughter: The Development of Nicola Barker's Grotesque Realism," 3: 87–97.

Schoene. Berthold. "Cosmo-Kitsch vs. Cosmopoetics," 3: 105–113.

Shaw, Katy. "(Dis)locations: Post-Industrial Gothic in David Peace's *Red Riding Quartet*," 3: 62–71.

Tomasula, Steve. "Many Makers Make Baby Post: 40 Years of Reading "The Babysitter"," 1: 219–234.

Vanderhaeghe, Stéphane. "Editor's Introductions: Well, Think of It This Way," 1: 15–16.

Waugh, Patricia. "Introduction," 3: 9–29.

Books Reviewed

Akutagawa, Ryunosuke. *A Fool's Life*, 3: 134–135. (David Cozy)

Baumbach, Jonathan. *Dreams of Molly*, 1: 291. (Robert Glick)

Becker, Daniel Levin. *Many Subtle Channels: In Praise of Potential Literature*, 2: 76–77. (Warren Motte)

Breckenridge, Donald. *This Young Girl Passing*, 1: 281–282. (Joseph Dewey)

Burch, Aaron. *How to Take Yourself Apart, How to Make Yourself Anew*, 2: 87. (Dylan Suher)

Burn, Stephen J. *David Foster Wallace's* Infinite Jest: *A Reader's Guide* (Second Edition), 3: 139–139. (David Ball)

Cohen, Joshua. *Four New Messages*, 2: 74–75. (Joseph Dewey)

Cooper, Dennis. *The Marbled Swarm,* 1: 280–281. (Jeremy M. Davies)

Daitch, Susan. *Paper Conspiracies*, 1: 295–296. (Pedro Ponce)

D'Annunzio, Gabriele. *Notturno*, 3: 129–130. (Brooke Horvath)

Darwish, Mahmoud. *In the Presence of Absence*, 1: 287–288. (Daniel Garrett)

de Eça de Queirós, José Maria. *The Correspondence of Fradique Mendes*, 2: 88. (Mark Axelrod)

des Forêts, Louis-René. *Poems of Samuel Wood*, 2: 79–80. (Erika Vause)

Draeger, Manuela. *In the Time of the Blue Ball*, 1: 286. (Levi Teal)

Dürenmatt, Friedrich and Max Frisch. *Correspondence*, 2: 88–89. (Richard Kalich)

Evenson, Brian. *Windeye*, 3: 131–132. (Ralph Clare)

Sontag, Susan. *As Consciousness is Harnessed to Flesh: Journals & Notebooks*, 3: 137–138. (Amy Kerner)

Taïa, Abdellah. *An Arab Melancholia*, 2: 84–85. (Amanda DeMarco)

Tulli, Magdalena. *In Red*, 1: 299–300. (Jeff Bursey)

Tusquets, Esther. *Seven Views of the Same Landscape*, 1: 286–287. (Levi Teal)

Ulay, Faruk. *Cultivation of Enigma*, 1: 292. (Norman Lock)

Vladislavić, Ivan. *A Labour of Moles*, 3: 128–129. (Michael Pinker)

—. *The Loss Library and Other Unfinished Stories*, 2: 83–84. (Michael Pinker)

Walser, Robert. *Berlin Stories*, 2: 81–82. (Michael Kinnucan)

Werfel, Franz. *Pale Blue Ink in a Lady's Hand*, 3: 135–136. (Michael Stein)

Williams, Diane. *Vicky Swanky Is a Beauty*, 1: 294–285. (Amanda DeMarco)

Wilson, Ada. *Red Army Faction Blues*, 1: 298–299. (Joseph Darlington)

Wittkop, Gabrielle. *The Necrophiliac*, 1: 293–294. (Yevgeniya Traps)

Wren, Jacob. *Revenge Fantasies of the Politically Dispossessed*, 2: 80. (A D Jameson)

Zambreno, Kate. *Green Girl*, 1: 297–298. (Lindsey Drager)

CONJUNCTIONS:59

Colloquy

Edited by
Bradford Morrow

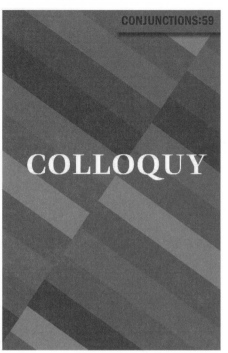

Begin your subscription with *Conjunctions:59, Colloquy* (November 2012). This astonishing issue includes an extensive selection of correspondence by the novelist William Gaddis, a collection of essays on monstrosity by China Miéville, Peter Straub, James Morrow, and others, and a portfolio of work about reading and writing, edited by Robert Coover and featuring contributions from William H. Gass, Lydia Davis, Shelley Jackson, Rosmarie Waldrop, and many more. Jonathan Lethem, Samuel R. Delany, Rae Armantrout, and numerous other contemporary masters and emerging voices complete this formidable anthology of never-before-published fiction, poetry, and creative nonfiction.

For information on the back issues from which you may choose your complimentary gift as part of this offer, visit our Archives at www.conjunctions.com/archive.htm. This offer also available for gift subscriptions.

CONJUNCTIONS
Edited by Bradford Morrow
Published by Bard College
Annandale-on-Hudson, NY 12504

To order, visit www.conjunctions.com
or e-mail conjunctions@bard.edu.

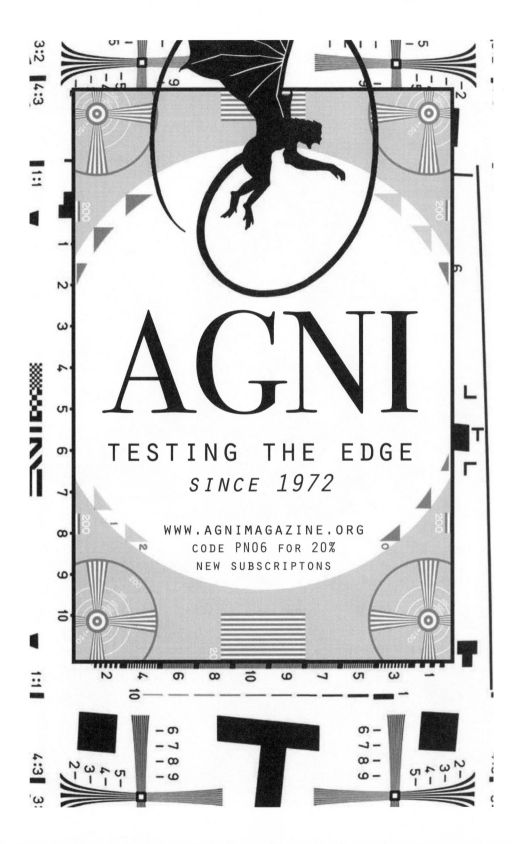

AGNI

TESTING THE EDGE

SINCE 1972

WWW.AGNIMAGAZINE.ORG
CODE PN06 FOR 20%
NEW SUBSCRIPTONS

NOON

A LITERARY ANNUAL

1324 LEXINGTON AVENUE   PMB 298   NEW YORK NY 10128

EDITION PRICE $12 DOMESTIC $17 FOREIGN

DELILLO FIEDLER GASS PYNCHON
University of Delaware Press
Collections on Contemporary Masters

UNDERWORDS
Perspectives on Don DeLillo's *Underworld*

Edited by Joseph Dewey, Steven G. Kellman, and Irving Malin

Essays by Jackson R. Bryer, David Cowart, Kathleen Fitzpatrick, Joanne Gass, Paul Gleason, Donald J. Greiner, Robert McMinn, Thomas Myers, Ira Nadel, Carl Ostrowski, Timothy L. Parrish, Marc Singer, and David Yetter

$39.50

INTO *THE TUNNEL*
Readings of Gass's Novel

Edited by Steven G. Kellman and Irving Malin

Essays by Rebecca Goldstein, Donald J. Greiner, Brooke Horvath, Marcus Klein, Jerome Klinkowitz, Paul Maliszewski, James McCourt, Arthur Saltzman, Susan Stewart, and Heide Ziegler

$35.00

LESLIE FIEDLER AND AMERICAN CULTURE

Edited by Steven G. Kellman and Irving Malin

Essays by John Barth, Robert Boyers, James M. Cox, Joseph Dewey, R.H.W. Dillard, Geoffrey Green, Irving Feldman, Leslie Fiedler, Susan Gubar, Jay L. Halio, Brooke Horvath, David Ketterer, R.W.B. Lewis, Sanford Pinsker, Harold Schechter, Daniel Schwarz, David R. Slavitt, Daniel Walden, and Mark Royden Winchell

$36.50

PYNCHON AND *MASON & DIXON*

Edited by Brooke Horvath and Irving Malin

Essays by Jeff Baker, Joseph Dewey, Bernard Duyfhuizen, David Foreman, Donald J. Greiner, Brian McHale, Clifford S. Mead, Arthur Saltzman, Thomas H. Schaub, David Seed, and Victor Strandberg

$39.50

ORDER FROM ASSOCIATED UNIVERSITY PRESSES
2010 Eastpark Blvd., Cranbury, New Jersey 08512
PH 609-655-4770   FAX 609-655-8366   E-mail AUP440@ aol.com

Dalkey Archive
Scholarly Series

Available Now

Approaching Disappearance
ANN McCONNELL

Robert Coover & the Generosity of the Page
STÉPHANE VANDERHAEGHE

Critical Dictionary of Mexican Literature
(1955–2010)
CHRISTOPHER DOMÍNGUEZ MICHAEL

Iranian Writers Uncencored:
Freedom, Democracy, and the Word in Contemporary Iran
SHIVA RAHBARAN

Pop Poetics
Reframing Joe Brainard
ANDY FITCH

Dumitru Tsepeneag and the Canon of
Alternative Literature
LAURA PAVEL

This Is Not a Tragedy:
The Works of David Markson
FRANÇOISE PALLEAU-PAPIN

The Birth of Death and Other Comedies:
The Novels of Russell H. Greenan
TOM WHALEN

When Blackness Rhymes with Blackness
ROWAN RICARDO PHILLIPS

A Community Writing Itself:
Conversations with Vanguard Writers of the Bay Area
SARAH ROSENTHAL, ED.

Aidan Higgins:
The Fragility of Form
NEIL MURPHY, ED.

Nicholas Mosley's Life and Art:
A Biography in Six Interviews
SHIVA RAHBARAN

The Subversive Scribe:
Translating Latin American Fiction
SUZANNE JILL LEVINE

Maurice Blanchot (1907–2003), one of the most influential figures of twentieth-century French literature, produced a wide
variety of essays and fictions that reflect on the complexities of
literary work. his description of writing continually returns to a
number of themes, such as solitude, passivity, indifference, anonymity, and absence—forces confronting the writer, but also the
reader, the text itself, and the relations between the three. For
Blanchot, literature involves a movement toward disappearance,
where one risks the loss of self; but such a sacrifice, says Blanchot, is inherent in the act of writing. *Approaching Disappearance*
explores the question of disappearance in Blanchot's critical work
and then turns to five narratives that offer a unique reflection on
the threat of disappearance and the demands of literature—work
by Franz Kafka, Jorge Luis Borges, Louis-René des Forêts, and
Nathalie Sarraute.

Approaching Disappearance

ANNE MCCONNELL

Dalkey Archive Scholarly Series
Literary Criticism
$34.95 / paper
ISBN: 978-1-56478-808-5

ANNE MCCONNELL

APPROACHING
DISAPPEARANCE

"*Approaching Disappearance* is an invigorating and intellectually mobile piece of work, one
that focuses boldly on the anxieties of contemporary literature, without compromise or
appeal to easy orthodoxy." —Warren Motte

Anne McConnell is an Assistant Professor in the English Department at West Virginia State University. She completed her
graduate work in Comparative Literature at the University of
Colorado at Boulder in 2006, specializing in twentieth-century
European and Hispanic literature and literary theory. She currently teaches world literature, literary criticism, and writing at
West Virginia State University.

Robert Coover and the Generosity of the Page is an unconventional study of Robert Coover's work from his early masterpiece *The Origin of the Brunists* (1966) to the recent Noir (2010). Written in the second person, it offers a self-reflexive investigation into the ways in which Coover's stories often challenge the reader to resist the conventions of sense-making and even literary criticism. By portraying characters lost in surroundings they often fail to grasp, Coover's work playfully enacts a "(melo)drama of cognition" that mirrors the reader's own desire to interpret and make sense of texts in unequivocal ways. this tendency in Coover's writing is in- dicative of a larger refusal of the ready-made, of the once-and-for-all or the authoritative, celebrating instead, in its generosity, the widening of possibilities—thus inevitably forcing the reader-critic to acknowledge the arbitrariness and artificiality of her responses.

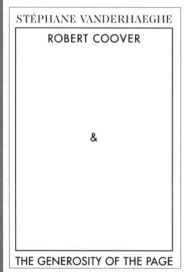

STÉPHANE VANDERHAEGHE

ROBERT COOVER

&

THE GENEROSITY OF THE PAGE

Robert Coover & the Generosity of the Page

Stéphane Vanderhaeghe

Dalkey Archive Scholarly Series
Cultural Studies
$34.95 / paper
ISBN: 978-1-56478-807-8

Stéphane Vanderhaeghe is Associate Professor at the University of Cergy-Pontoise, France, where he teaches American literature. His research focuses on contemporary, avant-garde writers and he has published essays on Robert Coover, Ben Marcus, or Shelley Jackson.

The Critical Dictionary of Mexican Literature from 1955 to the Present is both a personal anthology and a highly subjective and unscientific reference work, marrying the often acerbic, always poetic reviews and essays written on Mexican literature by renowned critic Christopher Domínguez Michael over the past thirty years to the quixotic ideal of a comprehensive dictionary of Mexico's recent literary history. With well over 150 entries, the Dictionary both introduces and interrogates the work of novelists, poets, essayists, and journalists working in Mexico between 1955 (date of the publication of Juan Rulfo's watershed Mexican Revolution novel Pedro Páramo) and the present day.

Critical Dictionary of Mexican Literature
(1955–2010)

CHRISTOPHER DOMÍNGUEZ MICHAEL
TRANSLATION BY
LISA DILLMAN

Dalkey Archive Scholarly Series
Literary Criticism
$29.95 / paper
ISBN: 978-1-56478-606-7

CRITICAL
DICTIONARY
OF MEXICAN
LITERATURE
(1955-2010)

CHRISTOPHER DOMÍNGUEZ MICHAEL

Christopher Domínguez Michael was born in Mexico City in 1962. He is a literary critic, historian of ideas, and novelist. He's a contributor to such prestigious periodicals as Vuelta, Letras Libres, and the literary supplement of the newspaper Reforma. His biography Vida de Fray Servando was awarded the Xavier Villaurrutia Prize in 2004, and one of his books on literary criticism (La sabiduría sin promesa) was awarded the international prize of the Art Circle of Santiago de Chile in 2009.

As poet Mohammad Hoghooghi says, "[Writing] constitutes resistance. Because, in any age, the poet has been a protestor of
a kind; resisting the thought-molds of the day. However, this
protest might be political, it might be social, or it might even be
philosophical. At any rate, the artist is at odds with the prevalent
conduct and thinking of his age; this has always been the case."
The 1979 Revolution in Iran was meant to bring freedom, hope,
and prosperity to an oppressed people, but the reality is well
known—the poets and writers interviewed by Shiva Rahbaran
in Iranian Writers Uncensored speak instead of humiliation, despotism, war, and poverty. These interviews with poets and writers still living and working in Iran demonstrate their belief that
literature's value is in opening spaces of awareness in the minds
of the reader—and pockets of freedom in society.

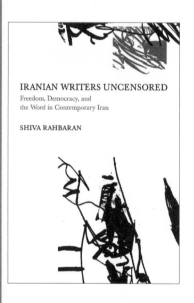

IRANIAN WRITERS UNCENSORED
Freedom, Democracy, and
the Word in Contemporary Iran

SHIVA RAHBARAN

Iranian Writers Uncencored:

Freedom, Democracy, and the Word
in Contemporary Iran

SHIVA RAHBARAN
TRANSLATION BY
NILOU MOBASSER

Dalkey Archive Scholarly Series
Cultural Studies
$17.95 / paper
ISBN: 978-1-56478-688-3

Shiva Rahbaran was born in 1970 in Tehran. She left Iran for
Germany in 1984, where she studied literature and political
science at the Heinrich-Heine-Universtät Düsseldorf. She continued her studies at Oxford University, where she was granted
a Ph.D. in English literature. She is also the author of Nicholas
Mosley's Life and Art: A Biography in Six Interviews and The
Paradox of Freedom, both published by Dalkey Archive Press.

Pop artists (painters and poets) often get praised or criticized for their use of low-brow commercial iconography. Yet either appraisal obscures the rigors of Pop serial design.

Adopting artist-poet Joe Brainard as its principal focus, this project presents Pop poetics not as a minor, coterie impulse meriting a sympathetic footnote in accounts of the postwar era's literary history, but as a missing link that potentially confounds any number of familiar critical distinctions (authentic record versus autonomous language, the "personal" versus the procedural). Pop poetics matter, argues Andy Fitch, not just to the occasional aficionado of Brainard's *I Remember*, but to anybody concerned with reconstructing the dynamic aesthetic exchange between postwar New York art and poetry.

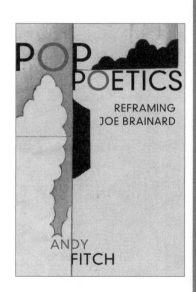

Pop Poetics
REFRAMING JOE BRAINARD

ANDY FITCH

Dalkey Archive Scholarly Series
Literary Criticism
$34.95 / paper
ISBN: 978-1-56478-728-6

Andy Fitch along with Jon Cotner, is the author of *Ten Walks / Two Talks*, which was chosen as a Best Book of 2010 by *Time Out Chicago*, The Millions, The Week, and Bookslut. He teaches in the MFA program at University of Wyoming.

It wasn't until after Dumitru Tsepeneag fled Romania for France in 1971 that he was able to speak frankly about the literary movement that he had helped create. "Oneiricism" wasn't just a new, homegrown form of surrealism, but implicitly a rebuke to the officially mandated socialist and nationalist realism imposed by Ceauşescu on all Romanian authors: here was writing devoted to the logic of dreams, not the grim reality policed by the communist regime. As such, *Dumitru Tsepeneag and the Canon of Alternative Literature* is not just the study of one man's work, but of an entire nation's literary history over the latter half of the twentieth century. The first monograph to appear in English on perhaps the most idiosyncratic and influential Romanian writer working today, *Dumitru Tsepeneag and the Canon of Alternative Literature* places Tsepeneag among the ranks of the great literary innovators—and pranksters—of the twentieth century.

DUMITRU TSEPENEAG AND THE CANON OF
ALTERNATIVE LITERATURE BY LAURA PAVEL

Dumitru Tsepeneag and the Canon of Alternative Literature

LAURA PAVEL
TRANSLATION BY
ALISTAIR IAN BLYTH

Dalkey Archive Scholarly Series
Literary Criticism
$23.95 / paper
ISBN: 978-1-56478-639-5

Laura Pavel is a Romanian essayist and literary critic. She is Associate Professor at the Faculty of Theater and Television of the Babeş-Bolyai University, and Head of the Department of Theater Studies and Media.

The very first book-length study to focus on this seminal American author, *This Is Not a Tragedy* examines David Markson's entire body of work, ranging from his early tongue-in-cheek Western and crime novels to contemporary classics such as *Wittgenstein's Mistress* and *Reader's Block*. Having begun in parody, Markson's writing soon began to fragment, its pieces adding up to a peculiar sort of self-portrait—doubtful and unsteady—and in the process achieving nothing less than a redefinition of the novel form. Written on the verge of silence, David Markson's fiction represents an intimate, unsettling, and unique voice in the cacophony of modern letters, and *This Is Not a Tragedy* charts Markson's attempts to find, in art and language, the solace denied us by life.

This Is Not a Tragedy:
The Works of David Markson

FRANÇOISE PALLEAU-PAPIN

Dalkey Archive Scholarly Series
Literary Criticism
$49.95 / paper
ISBN: 978-1-56478-607-4

THIS IS NOT A TRAGEDY **THE WORKS OF DAVID MARKSON**
FRANÇOISE PALLEAU-PAPIN

Françoise Palleau-Papin teaches American Literature at the Sorbonne Nouvelle University-Paris 3. She has edited a critical study of Patricia Eakins, and published articles on Willa Cather, Carole Maso, John Edgar Wideman, William T. Vollmann, and others.

Russell H. Greenan's *It Happened in Boston?* is one of the most radical narratives to appear in the late 1960s ("this is a book that encompasses everything," as David L. Ulin noted in *Bookforum*). Yet due in large part to the difficulty of classifying Greenan's fiction, many readers are unaware of his other novels. *In The Birth of Death and Other Comedies: The Novels of Russell H. Greenan*, Tom Whalen, drawing widely from the American literary tradition, locates Greenan's lineage in the work of Hawthorne and Poe, "where allegory and dream mingle with and illuminate realism," as well as in the fiction of Twain, West, Hammett, Cain, and Thompson. Examining Greenan's characteristic themes and strategies, Whalen provides perceptive readings of the dark comedies of this criminally neglected American master, and in a coda reflects on Greenan's career and the reception of his work.

The Birth of Death and Other Comedies:
The Novels of Russell H. Greenan

TOM WHALEN

Dalkey Archive Scholarly Series
Literary Criticism
$23.95 / paper
ISBN: 978-1-56478-640-1

Tom Whalen is a novelist, poet, translator and author of numerous stories and critical essays. He has written for *Agni, Bookforum, Film Quarterly, The Hopkins Review, The Iowa Review, The Literary Review, Studies in Short Fiction, The Wallace Stevens Journal*, the *Washington Post*, and other publications, and he co-edited the *Review of Contemporary Fiction*'s "Robert Walser Number."

In *When Blackness Rhymes with Blackness*, Rowan Ricardo Phillips pushes African-American poetry to its limits by unraveling "our desire to think of African-American poetry as African-American poetry." Phillips reads African-American poetry as inherently allegorical and thus a successful shorthand for the survival of a poetry but unsuccessful shorthand for the sustenance of its poems. Arguing in favor of the counterintuitive imagination, Phillips demonstrates how these poems tend to refuse their logical insertion into a larger vision and instead dwell indefinitely at the crux between poetry and race, where, when blackness rhymes with blackness, it is left for us to determine whether this juxtaposition contains a vital difference or is just mere repetition.

When Blackness Rhymes with Blackness

ROWAN RICARDO PHILLIPS

Dalkey Archive Scholarly Series
Literary Criticism
$25.95 / paper
ISBN: 978-1-56478-583-1

Rowan Ricardo Phillips's essays, poems, and translations have appeared in numerous publications. He is also the author of *The Ground* (2010). He has taught at Harvard, Columbia, and is currently Associate Professor of English and Director of the Poetry Center at Stony Brook University.

A Community Writing Itself features internationally respected writers Michael Palmer, Nathaniel Mackey, Leslie Scalapino, Brenda Hillman, Kathleen Fraser, Stephen Ratcliffe, Robert Glück, and Barbara Guest, as well as important younger writers Truong Tran, Camille Roy, Juliana Spahr, and Elizabeth Robinson. The book fills a major gap in contemporary poetics, focusing on one of the most vibrant experimental writing communities in the nation. The writers discuss vision and craft, war and peace, race and gender, individuality and collectivity, and the impact of the Bay Area on their work.

A Community
Writing Itself
Conversations
with Vanguard
Writers of the
Bay Area

Sarah Rosenthal in conversation with:
Michael Palmer **Nathaniel Mackey** Leslie Scalapino
Brenda Hillman Kathleen Fraser **Stephen Ratcliffe**
Robert Glück **Barbara Guest** Truong Tran
Camille Roy Juliana Spahr Elizabeth Robinson

A Community Writing Itself:

Conversations with Vanguard
Writers of the Bay Area

SARAH ROSENTHAL, ED.

Dalkey Archive Scholarly Series
Literature
$29.95 / paper
ISBN: 978-1-56478-584-8

"Sarah Rosenthal's interviews with some of the most engaging and important American poets of the time, all working in the Bay Area, provide vivid commentary on the state of the art and some of the most useful commentary available on the work of each individual writer."

—Charles Bernstein

Drawing together a wide range of focused critical commentary and observation by internationally renowned scholars and writers, this collection of essays offers a major reassessment of Aidan Higgins's body of work almost fifty years after the appearance of his first book, *Felo de Se*. Authors like Annie Proulx, John Banville, Derek Mahon, Dermot Healy, and Higgins himself, represented by a previously uncollected essay, offer a variety of critical and creative commentaries, while scholars such as Keith Hopper, Peter van de Kamp, George O'Brien, and Gerry Dukes contribute exciting new perspectives on all aspects of Higgins's writing. This collection confirms the enduring significance of Aidan Higgins as one of the major writers of our time, and also offers testament that Higgins's work is being rediscovered by a new generation of critics and writers.

Aidan Higgins:
The Fragility of Form

NEIL MURPHY, ED.

Dalkey Archive Scholarly Series
Literary Criticism
$29.95 / paper
ISBN: 978-1-56478-562-6

AIDAN HIGGINS:
THE FRAGILITY
OF FORM

*edited by Neil Murphy
with essays from*

ANNIE PROULX
JOHN BANVILLE
DERMOT HEALY
DEREK MAHON
GERRY DUKES
KEITH HOPPER
GEORGE O'BRIEN
PETER VAN DE KAMP
& AIDAN HIGGINS

Neil Murphy has previously taught at the University of Ulster and the American University of Beirut, and is currently Associate Professor of Contemporary Literature at NTU, Singapore. He is the author of several books on Irish fiction and contemporary literature and has published numerous articles on contemporary Irish fiction, on postmodernism, and on Aidan Higgins. He is currently writing a book on contemporary fiction and aesthetics.

The son of Sir Oswald Mosley, founder of the British Union of Fascists in the 1930s, and himself the inheritor of a noble title, Nicholas Mosley nonetheless fought bravely for Britain during World War II and became a tireless anti-apartheid campaigner thereafter, finding little sense in living the "hypocritical" life of a British aristocrat . . . and yet his numerous extramarital affairs came to shake not only the foundations of his marriage to his first wife, Rosemary, but also his growing sense of himself as a religious man.

The present biography is written in the form of six interviews, each focusing upon one aspect of Mosley's life—from his childhood and experiences as a young man, up to his reflections on religion, science, philosophy, and their impact on the political and ideological developments of our time.

Nicholas Mosley's Life and Art

a biography in six interviews
by shiva rahbaran

Nicholas Mosley's Life and Art:
A Biography in Six Interviews

SHIVA RAHBARAN

Dalkey Archive Scholarly Series
Literary Criticism
$25.95 / paper
ISBN: 978-1-56478-564-0

"Fascinating—Nicholas Mosley is the world's most brilliant conversationalist and this book catches the flavour of that."
—A. N. Wilson

To most of us, "subversion" means political subversion, but *The Subversive Scribe* is about collaboration not with an enemy, but with texts and between writers. Though Suzanne Jill Levine is the translator of some of the most inventive and revolutionary Latin American authors of the twentieth century—including Julio Cortázar, G. Cabrera Infante, Manuel Puig, and Severo Sarduy—here she considers the act of translation itself to be a form of subversion. Rather than regret translation's shortcomings, Levine stresses how translation is itself a creative act, unearthing a version lying dormant beneath an original work, and animating it, like some mad scientist, in order to create a text illuminated and motivated by the original. In *The Subversive Scribe*, one of our most versatile and creative translators gives us an intimate and entertaining overview of the tricky relationships lying behind the art of literary translation.

The Subversive Scribe:
Translating Latin American Fiction

SUZANNE JILL LEVINE

Dalkey Archive Scholarly Series
Literary Criticism
$13.95 / paper
ISBN: 978-1-56478-563-3

"A continually lively and very generous book, full of lore and such a vivid and just account of how complex a process good writing is."
SUSAN SONTAG

THE SUBVERSIVE SCRIBE
Translating Latin American Fiction
Suzanne Jill Levine

"A fascinating glimpse into the mental gyrations of a first-class literary translator at work."
—Clifford Landers, *Latin American Research Review*

ORDER FORM

Individuals may use this form to subscribe to the *Review of Contemporary Fiction* or to order back issues of the *Review* and Dalkey Archive titles at a discount (see below for details).

Title   ISBN   Quantity   Price

_____

_____

_____

_____

_____

_____

Subtotal _____

Less Discount _____
(10% for one book, 20% for two or more books, and
25% for Scholarly titles advertised in this issue)
Subtotal _____

Plus Postage _____
(U.S. $3 + $1 per book; foreign $7 + $5 per book)

1 Year Individual Subscription to the **Review** _____
($17 U.S.; $22.60 Canada; $32.60 all other countries)

Total _____

Mailing Address _____

_____

_____

_____

Credit card payment   ☐ Visa   ☐ Mastercard

Acct. # _____ Exp. date _____

Name on card _____ Phone # _____

Billing zip code _____

Please make checks (in U.S. dollars only) payable to *Dalkey Archive Press.*

mail or fax this form to: Dalkey Archive Press, University of Illinois,
1805 S. Wright Street, MC-011, Champaign, IL 61820
fax: 217.244.9142 tel: 217.244.5700